COMET'S FIRST CHRISTMAS

The North Pole Chronicles: Book One

DELILAH NIGHT

Copyright © 2021 by Delilah Night

All rights reserved.

No part of this book may be reproduced in any form or by any electronic or mechanical means, including information storage and retrieval systems, without written permission from the author, except for the use of brief quotations in a book review.

ASIN : B0989446DH

Cover Design: Shakil Awan

For Elanor

Chapter One

*P*ulling Santa's sleigh is as prestigious as it gets. When I trained as a potential team member, I knew the odds of ever actually pulling the sleigh were low. But I did let myself fantasize about how one day there would be a knock at my door, and Rudolph would be there to call me up.

Never once did I picture it happening in December.

That would be absurd.

I was studying in human form when the doorbell to my home rang. It was probably my mom, trying to get me to date some friend's daughter. I went to the door, expecting a guilt trip and "the perfect woman" for me to date and eventually produce little calves with for my mother to spoil. I nabbed a handful of hay and took a big mouthful before I nudged the door open with my foot.

It wasn't my mother.

The reindeer who'd pawed at my door was Rudolph. *Rudolph!* She wasn't wearing any regalia, but I'd been a huge fan for years. She used to be Prancer, but became Rudolph when the previous Rudolph retired—job titles were permanent, the people filling those positions were not.

I realized I was (a) staring and (b) had a mouth full of hay.

"Excuse me," I mumbled through the hay, and I hastily ate it. I wished I was in my reindeer form—my human face was burning with humiliation.

"Claudia?"

I forced down the last gulp of hay, feeling the less well-chewed bits scrape my throat as the unpleasant bite made its way down my gullet.

"Y—yes? Am I in trouble?"

Had I posted something online that was in poor taste? Had I done something to disqualify myself as a potential team member? My brain seized up with anxiety, and I couldn't find a clear thought.

Rudolph laughed. "No, that was my first thought when I was called up, too, though."

Wait, what? Called up?

"Excuse me?" I was so confused.

"Claudia, you're being *called up*. You're being asked to help guide the sleigh. Comet can't fly this year," Rudolph said.

The world both turned to static. It made my brain pulse.

"Calling me up?" My voice sounded far away, and the world suddenly went from static into stark relief. Nothing made sense. Nothing.

Rudolph whuffed in irritation. "Yes, calling you up. Report to the barn in an hour. Unless you're not interested…" Her voice trailed off, and she tossed her antlers.

"I am! I am interested!" I had to get it out before the opportunity was taken away from me. "I want to!"

Rudolph snorted with amusement. "Okay, you want to

do it. Good. Report to the barn in an hour," she repeated and left. Before she got too far from my door, she turned back. "You're going to want to hurry up. Only twenty-three days left until the Big Show." She leapt in the air and bounded away.

Each thought melted like a snowflake on the tongue, disappearing too fast, replaced by the next. *I'm going to join the team! Oh my God, there's only just over three weeks until Christmas! What if I let Santa down?*

I sagged against the doorframe. A team member.

I confess I spent some of the next hour grooming my reindeer form. I made sure my antlers weren't jagged, that my coat was glossy, and that my hooves were polished. Then I left for Reindeer Complex.

The barn loomed large in my memories. Like most calves, I'd toured it during the January to June slow season when Santa, Mrs. Claus, and most of the team were off doing whatever they did in those six months of the year. I'd watched practices, hoping for an autograph. As a potential, I'd learned to shift and to fly there. Part of me still held my breath when I walked through the doors—and now I'd be entering the inner sanctum.

A blue-skinned snowman, over a head taller than my human form, t-shirt stretching over big muscles was guarding the entrance. Like the other security guards, he wore black. I immediately felt doubt. What if I'd hallucinated the whole encounter with Rudolph?

"Hi. I'm Claudia? I'm supposed to be replacing Comet this year?" I couldn't keep my uncertainty out of my voice.

"Scan your hoof," the snowman said, gesturing to the scanner.

I did as I was told, and the snowman opened the door to the barn. "Have a good day, Comet."

Comet.

That was going to take some getting used to. If I ever could get used to it, that is.

The barn was swirling chaos. There must have been some order to it, but I couldn't see it. All I saw was a tidal wave of elves.

"Comet!" One of the elves peeled away from the group and approached me. She was roughly my human form's height with a long curly ponytail. Her jeans and green t-shirt were standard wear for the elves in the barn. Toymakers could wear what they wanted as long as it had red. Administration were assigned silver and Personal Assistants wore gold. "Glad you're here. We have to get you up to speed. Let's go see Blitzen."

The elf was already walking away. I bounded after her to catch up. She led me down several halls into what I knew were the personal stalls the team used, each labeled with a brass name plate. They had been described to the potentials as personal offices with equipment for use in both forms. Most of the stalls seemed to have crowds of elves around them. She led me to the third stall on the left —one of only two without elves—and banged on the door. I glanced at the sign—*Blitzen*.

"She's in here. Good luck," the elf said and walked away.

"Wait! Aren't you going to stay?" I called after her.

The door to the stall was yanked open. A tall, thin woman with a blonde braid opened the door. "I told you I didn't want to be interrupted until *after* I—" she stopped and looked me over. "Oh, it's you. Okay, Comet, you need an upgraded I.D., phone, email account, and a Naughty-or-Nice login."

"Hi. My name's Claudia," I said.

"Your name should be Athena with your test scores, Comet. Ironic, since the only one of us who had higher marks at your age was Comet." She paused and flipped the braid over her shoulder. "This is going to get confusing. You can be Kid Comet. Come on in."

"Um, I'd prefer Clau—" I began.

"While I'm getting your tech sorted," she continued as if I hadn't spoken at all, "you should talk to Comet. This is her—your—year in the Eastern North America region. It was Cupid's region last year, so you'll have her notes. Comet has been working with the various elves to plan her route for this year, so she'll be a good resource for you. Lots of the Nicest in your region, and you have some population heavy cities—New York is a workout by itself. Anyways, lots for you to catch up on."

I tried to absorb what she was saying, but all I was really catching was *Kid Comet*, *Eastern North America* and *talk to Comet*.

To deal with the mental overload, I looked around the room, following the advice I'd found online.

Five things you see: Okay—hay, computer screen in the wall, human-sized desk with another computer, big comfy chair, fishbowl full of—dice?—weird-shaped dice.

Four things you can feel: I could feel the floor under my hooves, a slight ache in my left front hoof where I cut the nail a bit too far, the rug when I stepped on it, and whether it should technically count or not, I could feel Blitzen's eyes on me.

Three things you can hear: I could hear my heart roaring in my chest, elves shouting in the hallway, and Blitzen's shifted form's fingers clacking on a keyboard as she typed.

Two things you can smell: I could smell the fresh hay in the feeder , and the stale coffee on Blitzen's desk.

One thing I can taste: I didn't have gum or anything to shove in my mouth. But I could taste a faint metallic taste.

"Doing okay, there?" Blitzen asked warily.

"I'm just a little overwhelmed."

"Of course you are!" A very pregnant woman entered the room. "Zen, did you just start doing your tech babble at her, or did you take five minutes to get to know her?"

Blitzen turned a little pink. "She needs her N-o-N login and stuff."

"Let me guess, you're Claudia?" the newcomer said to me.

I nodded.

"I'm Comet, but you can call me Wendy. Most of us answer to either our real name or our title. With some exceptions, right, Zen?"

"We are twenty-three days out, so maybe we should care more about the N-o-N login and less about my first name."

"Her name is Persephone, but we—"

"But we call me Zen all the time," Zen said with an air of finality.

"Of course," I answered both of them.

"I was talking to Natalia outside and I heard you steamrolling Claudia. Don't worry, honey, you'll have all of my notes, Cupid's notes from last year, and a Personal Assistant in the region who will help you. And it's not *that* many gifts. These days, Santa only has to personally deliver a fraction of the top percentage of the Nicest. Our parents' generation had to pull the full weight of the sleigh to *every* believer. My back hurts just thinking about it. We're lucky he uses the beam thingy you invented for most of them."

"It's a *transporter*, not a 'beam thingy.' Wait, shouldn't you be in the hospital wing?" Blitzen's eyes widened.

My eyes went to Comet's belly. She did look awfully pregnant. A large soccer ball-sized belly stretched her red and white sweater to the limit. Was she going to give birth *now*? Calving season wasn't for four months. Had she somehow triggered the parthenogenesis in the wrong month? And if they had known she was pregnant, why was I only promoted today?

Comet laughed. "Be careful, Zen, or I might think you care. I'm here to help Claudia get set up a little before I leave. Christine is going to hover over me when I get home. I'm enjoying the last few moments before I have to rest. Oh, and Wei Liang asked me to give you a message."

"A message? Isn't he supposed to be helping me?" Blitzen protested.

"He said he wanted a break from you because, and I quote, 'How do you stand her bitching about Christmas?'" she replied. "He'll meet up with you in Singapore next week."

I gasped. "You don't like *Christmas*?"

"I don't hate Christmas; you all love it too much!" Zen snapped. "I'm happy to join in a rousing chorus of Jingle Bells during my extracurricular hours, but I want to be able to hear myself think when I'm working."

Wendy's eyes glittered with mischief. "If you think that's scandalous, you should ask Zen about her last girlfriend, who didn't even believe."

I gasped. "How is that possible?"

"Humans, both reindeer answered in unison. Wendy looked amused. Zen smirked a *been there done that, got the t-shirt* smile.

I almost asked them how they had the time to date, but I was worried they might actually tell me, so I kept my mouth shut.

"Don't look so scandalized," Zen said. "Once you leave the Pole, they're everywhere. Comet, you should rest. Kid Comet will be fine."

"Or just call her Claudia," the real Comet—Wendy—

said. She put an arm on my back and led me into the hall. "Zen, bring her stuff to her when you're ready with it. Please write out any helpful details in actual human languages and not your nerd languages."

"Learning new languages trains the brain," Zen retorted with another smirk.

"I speak every language spoken on Earth. I don't need to learn Dothraki and Klingon to satisfy you." Wendy looked at me and quirked a brow. "Do you speak any nerd languages?"

I quickly shook my head, careful of my antlers. I wasn't sure I knew any languages at that moment in time, but I wasn't about to admit it.

"You're all buzzkills," Zen said with an eyeroll. "Let me work."

As we walked down the hall, Wendy was regularly stopped.

First was an elf pulling a load of hay. "Comet! How are you feeling?"

"I'm feeling like somewhere between a house and an elephant. Twins. That's not supposed to happen," Wendy said with an air of shock and a little pride.

"Twins? That's definitely cause for celebration. And now the team change makes sense." The elf turned to me. "New Comet?"

I bobbed my head.

"Nice to meet you."

The next stall had a name plate which read *Prancer*. I saw her in human form—they were all in human form, it seemed—doing one handed push-ups. I remembered she was the team's trainer. Would she think I'd done a good enough job at keeping my muscles fit?

"Caity!" Wendy called.

Prancer—Caity, I guess I could call her—jumped to

her feet, grabbed a towel and came to the door. "Hey, mama. I heard the bad news. How are you feeling?" Her attention fell on me. I looked into kind green eyes. "Let me guess—you're our new Comet?"

"This is Claudia." Wendy introduced me.

"Hi, kiddo. I got the reports on you from Janine." Janine was the trainer for the five of us who were currently serving as potentials. I adored her, and hoped I'd made her proud. "She said you could do a little more exercise in human form. I've got a list of things you can do, and I'll send it to your new email once Zen gets it hooked up.

"Am I supposed to be in human form right now?" I asked. Increasingly, I was feeling like I'd failed my first test. But Rudolph had been in reindeer form, so I'd thought I was supposed to be, too. Maybe it was an indoors thing?

They are going to figure out that I'm an imposter any second.

Wendy shrugged. "Whatever at this point, right, Caity?"

"Yeah, don't stress it. But while I've got you here—I've been updating the team best practices for your conditioning during pregnancy and recovery. We've never dealt with twins, so don't do any of the exercises before your doctors and I have a long chat, Wendy. I have some ideas, though. I jotted down—let me grab them for you."

Wendy trilled a laugh. "Caity, I love you, but I'm going to be lying in front of my screens and I'm going to be streaming human entertainment until these kids come out, and then I'll be too busy with *twins* to be thinking of conditioning for a while. If I get bored, I'll help Rudolph with paperwork or something."

"But…fitness is important," Caity said, sounding almost sad.

"Not happening, Coach Prancer."

Caity blushed. "Catch you when you're back, Claudia."

Wendy led me onward.

"Prancer—Caity—said 'when I come back.' Why would she say that?"

Wendy closed her eyes. "Oh, honey, this is happening all out of order. I had a plan and it's gone all to hell. I can fly pregnant with one calf, but not two. I was supposed to be heading to New York today, flying on the team this year, and then you would be notified on December twenty-sixth, giving you a full year to prepare for next year's Big Show. But *surprise*," she waved her hands in the air, "it's twins and I'm officially too pregnant to fly."

"I'm going to New York? Is someone coming with me?"

"You're going to go alone, Claudia, but you'll have the New York team backing you. I saved New York so I could do the whole Christmas in New York thing—go to shows, window shop, ice skate, all that jazz. You're going to be in meetings a lot of the time—they need to get you up to speed—but the closer we get to the Big Show, the stronger your Christmas Magic will be. You'll find that you process the data so much faster. After studying humans and their various cultures for so long, I'm sure you'll want to explore and experience things for yourself. I hope you'll use my tickets to see *Nutcracker*, and that Jillian will ensure you have some fun. Simulations only teach you so much about what the real world is like."

We came to the office labeled *Comet*. Elves were packing up Wendy's possessions.

"You don't need to get rid of your stuff. I can manage." I was a little dismayed at how fast the elves were working.

"You'll want to put your own touch on the office and it's yours for at least two Christmases." She patted my spine. "Excuse me, but we need the office for about an hour at most." she said to the elves.

"Sure, Comet." One elf gestured and they all left.

"So let's review shifting," Wendy said.

I took three deep breaths, thought *human*, and allowed my body to morph from reindeer to human. I sported a red fashionable sweater and leggings so dark a green they were a hair's breadth away from black. Wendy broke out into a smile. She shifted to reindeer, then when she was human her clothes were different. I copied her.

"Excellent. Now show me what you'd choose to wear in New York. Remember it's cold there and humans react to cold differently."

I thought back to my classes, and to the human movies I'd seen. I morphed into a human wearing jeans, a sweater, and a black peacoat with a purple scarf around my neck and a matching hat with a little pom-pom on top. I glanced at my feet, frowned, and changed the sneakers to boots.

"Perfect. I think you're ready from my side of things. Zen should be here any minute with your tech. Once that's all sorted, you'll be off!"

Off. She made it sound so simple. I'd never actually left the Pole. What would it be like? Smell like? Taste like? Excitement zinged through my body, followed by fear shivering along the same paths. Would I embarrass myself? Would I look like a—what was the word?—rube? Would this Jillian be able to tell that I was a phony?

"Did I hear you invoking the name of the great and powerful Zen?"

Wendy rolled her eyes. "Are you dialing it up to eleven to impress the kid or to terrorize her?"

The kid. I'm twenty-five human years old!

"I'm being fun," Zen said breezily.

Wendy snorted.

Zen handed me a laptop, several printed sheets, and a cellphone. "Use the laptop and follow the instructions on the top page to set up permanent passwords for your N-o-N login and email. Then follow the instructions on the next page to configure your phone. It's basically two phones in one. It has a human mode for when you're around humans. It will look just like a regular human phone. Then you can use your magic to unlock Pole mode, which has access to the N-o-N, your Pole email, and everything we don't want people to see. Make sure you know how to move between the two. That's important. We've had people with the special phones get mugged, or lose their purse or whatever. A human can't see a phone in Pole mode in action. We serve the believers, we don't expose Christmas Magic. Take some time and explore everything while I razz Comet about being too knocked up to fly."

Wendy let loose a peal of laughter. "You know you're missing me already."

"You do know how to keep the flight from getting tedious," Comet agreed. "Hey, Kid Comet?"

"Yes?" God, now I was *answering* to Kid Comet? "And please can it be Claudia?"

"Fine. Claudia. Are you fun? Will you help keep me from boredom?"

Boredom? On the night of the Big Show? How was that possible? I guess Zen had been on the team for over a decade. Maybe it wasn't as magical to her now. I couldn't imagine not thinking it was the most exciting thing ever. I couldn't *wait* to fly. When I wasn't nauseous for fear of screwing it all up, that is.

"I'm not an expert on Klingon, but I read a lot of books. I read one you might like?" I felt a little exposed. I didn't give book recommendations easily. And if Blitzen hated my recommendation, would she think I was stupid?

But based on knowing her for less than an hour, I had a good feeling. "It's a take on King Arthur in space. It's called *Once & Future*. If you're interested, I can lend you my copy."

Zen's face broke out in a huge smile. "By Amy Rose Capetta and Cori McCarthy. It's an excellent book. Okay, you pass. You're fun, or at least you have the potential to be fun."

I turned my attention to the paperwork. Using my Christmas Magic, I had mastery over the N-o-N system, had set up my email, and learned how to configure my phone (and loaded it with books) in only twenty minutes or so. Wendy was sitting in the armchair, while Zen sat at her feet. I heard laughter more than once, and when I looked up, I realized that what they'd always told us about the team was true—they were a family. Wendy might be super maternal, and Zen snarky, but they fit together in a way I didn't think I ever would. It was like they had smooth edges that came together perfectly, and I was nothing but jagged edges when it came to fitting in.

Wendy took a call in the hallway. When she came back, she had a regretful look. "I'm being summoned home so my wife and my friend—"

Zen interrupted. "Your friend who is supposed to be my Personal Assistant this year."

Wendy tugged on Zen's braid. "Wei Liang will see you next week. That's soon enough. As I was saying, so they can make sure I'm not taxing myself too much. Can you take it from here? She just needs to know her schedule and where she's going."

"Sure. Take care. I'll come by to visit in a few days. I have to say, though—growing an extra kid just to get extra presents seems a bit excessive. Just saying."

Having seen the love and the relationship between

them, I started to get Zen. Zen showed her care and compassion with snark. And in my case, the stupid nickname wasn't to put me in my place, the way I'd feared. It was an attempt to make me feel like I fit in.

"Whatever, *Persephone*. Claudia, call me tonight. We'll videochat and I can advise you while you're gone," Wendy said. She came over and gave me a warm hug. "You can do this. We called you up because you're the right woman for the job."

And then with a hug for Zen, Wendy left the stall. I looked at Zen, not sure what she wanted me to do.

"So, what questions do you have?" Zen asked.

I had made notes, and asked my questions about the N-o-N system, hoping they weren't basic or stupid. But Zen seemed happy to explain, patiently helping me until I was ready to go.

"You're going to forty-eight West 77th Street. Land on the roof. When you do, you'll see two doors. Which one do you pick?"

I knew the answer to this test. "The one that's obviously shrouded with Christmas Magic. It will be slightly out of focus."

"Exactly right. The head of the office is Jillian. She'll get you up to speed and is your Personal Assistant this year. She can handle it—she's been head elf for the region for the past five years."

"Does she speak Klingon?" I teased before I thought of it. Mortified I slapped a hand over my mouth.

Zen just laughed. "Nah, none of them do. More's the pity."

"Do you really take notes in Klingon, or do you just tell everyone you do?" I was genuinely curious, and Zen seemed like the type who might use a rumor to her advantage.

"Oh, I do. Here's the deal. I fell in love with the human show Star Trek when I was a kid. I loved the idea of the Klingons, so I asked for a Klingon dictionary. Unlike human languages, which I just know, I had to work to learn it. So I value it a little more highly, and I take notes in it."

"But then aren't you the only person who can read them?"

"I'd translate them for the right person, but that person hasn't materialized." Zen grinned.

"Can you tell me a bit more about Jillian?"

"Jillian is one of the best! I worked with her two years ago when I did East North America. Some Personal Assistants have a certain way of doing stuff and because it's their region, and we need to be flexible and adjust to their way of doing things. Jillian tries to be the flexible one in New York and accommodate our way of doing things. Especially since it's your first year, she'll try to ensure that you feel supported. She's respectful of boundaries, so tell her what you need. I worked well with her; she turned down the Christmas music to give me quiet, she got me human coffee, and she adjusted her approach to working with me as we got used to each other. I don't mean this as an insult to Wei Liang, but this year *I* have to be the flexible one, and Singapore's elves go all in on Christmas."

"Why be on the team if you don't like Christmas?"

Zen looked scandalized. "Miss out on the Big Show? I love flying. I love doing the tech and helping the Pole that way. Look, I don't dislike Christmas. I *love* Christmas. I just wish that now and then it could be dialed back to like an eight from the eleven everyone else keeps it at." She snorted. "Santa's cool with my feelings on that. And, true story, there's a reason he goes on vacation with Mrs. Claus from the twenty-seventh of December until July—he likes a break from the Christmas of it all, too. But don't worry

—you do you. If you want to enjoy Christmas at a fourteen, take it there."

I nodded.

"Ready to go, Kid Comet?"

"Yes. But hey, much as I like that you want to make me feel included, could we keep that nickname between us?"

Zen smiled. "Sure. Just like Wally West became the Flash, you will transcend Kid Comet and become Comet."

I shook my head. Zen led me to the field, watched me morph to reindeer form, and walked me to what we all called the runway. I took a deep breath and looked at the sky. I was going to fly for real, and not just within the bounds of the Pole or in a simulation.

"I know we could transport you and have you there in an instant. But it's better for you to get the practice, and I bet you're dying to fly outside of a simulation of the world."

I glanced around and was relieved there were no fans to watch me leave. I didn't want to jump into the air and then fall on my butt in front of an audience. "I can't wait!"

Zen scratched right between my antlers and I whuffed with pleasure. "You've got this."

I nodded my head. I took a deep breath, and with my ever-present anxiety twisting into my excitement, I leaped into the air. I was on my first official mission!

Chapter Two

Flying was like opening a present—picking up something I've been dreaming about for so long and *finally* seeing what lay beneath the paper, or, in my case, outside the Pole. I put up a sight shield to make myself invisible to human eyes the moment just before I passed through the barrier to the human world. Everything on this side was so different from our training simulations. Even the air tasted different, like the myriad possibilities gave it a tang. The wind sang in my ears as I galloped past Winnipeg to Chicago. I was so tempted to land and try that whole "deep dish pizza" thing I'd heard of for lunch, but I didn't have access to money yet, and the New York office was expecting me before dinner. I had to settle for taking deep breaths, and I was slightly embarrassed and disappointed when I couldn't smell anything this far up, because of course I couldn't. From Chicago I turned East. I did a slight detour to fly over Detroit and Cleveland, to get a reindeer's eye view of the cities.

I felt both the thrill of excitement and the call of adventure when I saw the iconic New York City skyline. I flew low to get a good view of the Statue of Liberty, then did a pass over Manhattan from the Cloisters to the Battery. The people below me were tiny as ants. What would they think if they looked up and could see me? Would we suddenly have an influx of believers like in *Elf* or would I be a terrifying sight? I soared over Central Park, and I wished I could see it at its greenest even as I found the white mounded snow comforting and familiar. I could have spent all day and all night flying over the city, seeing all the sights from up high, but instead I searched out the address Zen had given me. I landed and morphed to human shape.

From the roof I could see The Museum of Natural History and Central Park. I could hear the sounds of the city I'd only heard in media, although it was not the cacophony I'd been led to think it would be. I took a bracing gulp of air, but still couldn't taste anything other than the ice in the air. I was so eager to try all the new things.

Focus. You're on a job. The job—the one you've been dreaming of your whole life. Don't screw up.

As promised, there were two entrances from the roof, and one was blurry. That was my door. I knocked. The door opened and an elf moved to the side, leaving the doorway unblocked. I stepped inside and dropped my sight shield.

"Comet! Nice to meet you, I'm Geena," said the elf. She…was not wearing silver. Had they forgotten to tell us that elves outside the Pole don't use our color designations? I'd expect someone in administration to be wearing the customary silver. Instead, she had on black skinny jeans, a pink top, and her blue hair was in an adorable pixie cut. She looked cute, but she didn't look like any elf I'd ever seen. But she was here, and she knew I was Comet, so I decided to go with it.

Fish flopped in my stomach as I extended my hand. "I'm Claudia," I said.

"Welcome. I'm going to introduce you to Jillian, your P.A. She's excited to help you. We all are! We want the Eastern North America route to go off without a hitch, so we are all at your disposal and ready to help with anything you need." Geena led me down a hallway. Someone must have just baked because I could smell fresh gingerbread in the air. I had to swallow to keep from drooling at the scent.

"Someone has been baking," I commented. I wondered if I could make the argument that gingerbread was something I *needed*.

"In your honor! We hope you like gingerbread. By the time we thought to ask, you'd left the Pole. If you don't like it, we can bake something fresh or send out for something. We know it's your first assignment, so you probably want to try a lot of things while you're here."

"That's—" I was mortified to feel tears prick the backs of my eyes at the gratitude welling up. "That's really kind. I love gingerbread."

"Zoe! Grab Comet a plate of gingerbread!" Geena called. Someone deeper in the apartment yelled back in the affirmative.

"You'll probably want to get your bearings and settle in tonight?" She glanced at me, and smiled when I nodded. They knew how this worked far better than I did, so I thought it was probably better to just follow their lead.

The Pole owned the building. The first floor through the fifteenth were apartments for the elves residing in New York, and some meeting rooms. The penthouse was a combination office/apartment that took up the whole floor.

Jillian and other high-ranking elves worked in the offices, and there was a bedroom for me.

"I'll give you the quick tour," Geena said, leading me past open rooms where people were working. "You'd normally find me, Jillian, and about ten other elves in these offices, but with the delegations here to plan the route, it's gotten a bit crowded."

As we walked down the hall, I heard Christmas music, playing at a low volume. No vocals, just a solo piano. It was a low-key approach that Zen would probably approve of.

"We have an office set aside for you. Comet—the other Comet—was only planning to work in human form. Is that okay? If you want a stall office, we can try to pull something together—the sleeping stall set aside for you can convert to an office, but usually—"

"A human office sounds fine," I said. The reindeer I'd run into in the barn back at the Pole were all in human form, and I could type faster and more accurately than the voice recognition system could. Zen was great, but even she couldn't make a perfect voice typing app.

I followed Geena from the office section of the penthouse into the open plan living room/kitchen. I stopped dead in my tracks at the sight of twenty elves who turned and hit me with a tsunami of variants on "Hi, Comet!" My first instinct was to turn and flee. I could feel the rising panic, and my breathing started to speed up.

I managed to register that, like Geena, these were not the elves I was used to at the Pole. They could have been human. Some were bustling around the warmly lit kitchen while others were seated at the sparkling black granite breakfast bar chatting among themselves. Three bakers were moving confidently through the kitchen debating something—oooh, would they make peppermint bark next? There was a group huddled together in a corner, working on laptops. One elf was seated at the upright piano—the source of the music I'd heard earlier.

There was so much diversity in clothing and hair color that I had no choice but to see them all as individuals, rather than the jobs they'd do for the Pole. For the first time I questioned the formality around clothing, and the way uniforms robbed people of individuality. On one hand, sure I knew the job of every elf based on their clothes, but they were mostly interchangeable to me. I needed to make more of an effort to get to know the elves around me, not just here but at the Pole as well.

I took three calming breaths, and raised a hand to awkwardly wave at them. "Hi, everyone. I look forward to working with you." I was relieved to hear my tone seemed to sound calm and professional, even though I felt overwhelmed and wanted to hide.

"This is the living room and kitchen. There's also a dining room through there."

I took in the white walls covered in photos in stark black frames of both the elves and team members going back at least two decades. I saw one of a younger Wendy as well as more recent Zen and Cupid images.

"We hope you'll pose for a picture before you leave," Geena said, noticing where my eyes had gone.

"Um, okay," I managed.

The golden wood floors gleamed as if they'd been waxed in my honor (I hope they hadn't gone through such a hassle for me). There was a big television mounted opposite the kitchen, the comfy looking green couch where elves argued good-naturedly about a call in the Rangers/Redwings game faced it. About them were strewn silver and gold tasseled throw pillows and a couple of very soft-looking blankets. I'm not sure what I had expected. Maybe something very minimalistic and basic.

This, though… This was a real apartment, decorated like a home.

Along one of the walls were huge picture windows overlooking the city. The sunset behind the skyscrapers painted a picture I'd hold with me forever—the buildings gleaming in the dying sunlight, their glass surfaces throwing back reflections of the pinks and purples smeared across the sky.

Someone in the kitchen yelled out, "Does Comet want hot cocoa or peppermint tea or candy cane coffee?"

"Cocoa please, with extra marshmallows," I requested. That was what my mom always gave me when I was anxious at home.

Geena called back my request with a grin. "Okay, let's see… I can show you the sleeping stall and bedroom now or Jillian can show you later if you want to jump into work."

"I think I'd like to meet Jillian first."

Geena nodded, and led me back down the hall toward the offices. She knocked at a door. "Jillian? Comet is here."

"Come in," called the voice.

The door swung open and I swear that my heart just…stopped.

Jillian gave us a dazzling smile and stood. She had also abandoned the official Pole attire rules, but I couldn't be bothered to care. Not when her blue eyes sparkled at me. Not when those plump lips curved in a smile. Not when I was wondering if her blonde hair felt as silky as it looked.

"Comet, welcome! I'm Jillian"

"Hi, I'm Clau—Comet," I said. The other elf ignored my name for my job title, so why wouldn't Jillian? Reindeer continuously changed regions, so even if they all called me Claudia in Eastern North America, next year I'd have to start from scratch with the new set of elves in my next region. Maybe this is why the team generally went by their titles?

Jillian took my offered hand in both of hers and held it for a moment as she continued to speak. "Thank you for coming last minute like this. We understand it's a lot to take in. We are fully prepared to get you ready for the Big Show. We have every faith in you."

My hand had started tingling when she touched it—as if a champagne bottle had been popped in my hand. Bubbles fizzed throughout my hand, and up my arm like a delicious toast to New Year's Eve. I licked my suddenly dry lips.

"—than gingerbread?" Jillian finished and looked at me expectantly.

"Sorry?" My face burned with mortification. She'd been talking and I'd been objectifying her.

"I asked if you were hungry for more than gingerbread," Jillian said. "It must all be overwhelming."

"That's certainly one word for it," I said with a wry smile.

Geena brought the gingerbread and cocoa to me. "Here you go, Comet. Jillian, please let me know where you want food from today. Henry and I are scheduled to leave in twenty minutes or so."

I took a bite and my eyes closed in pleasure. "This is amazing."

"Thank you! Laurel will be so happy to hear you liked it," Geena said. "Well, I'll leave you to it."

"Thank you, Geena," Jillian said, dismissing the other elf.

I glanced at my gingerbread and realized Jillian didn't have any. "Do you want some of this?"

"No, I'm saving room in my stomach for dinner. I've been craving pizza all day."

"Like New York style pizza?" I gasped with delight. Then I realized where I was and what I'd said, covered my face with my hands, and groaned. "I sound like an idiot. Ignore me, please."

"I wasn't going to get it from anywhere special. Is there a specific pizza place you want to eat at in the city?"

I shook my head. "I only know what I've seen on tv and in movies. If you like it, then I'll probably like it." If she said she loved remodeling, I'd have a sudden addiction to HGTV.

She cocked her head at me. "Do you want to go out and get pizza instead of ordering in?"

Every muscle in my body went on high alert. "Yes! Can we? Please?" I was trying not to squeal, but my voice was getting very high pitched.

Jillian pressed her lips together, clearly trying to repress a smile.

"It's okay, you can laugh," I said ruefully, my face burning.

"I would never laugh at you. It's your first time out of the Pole. Of course you're going to want to explore and have experiences. I know Comet had planned to come here because she wanted the quintessential Christmas in New York experience. I planned all of that out for her—would you like to follow that plan, too?"

I nodded eagerly.

"Okay, give me a minute to confer with the team to figure out the best pizza place to take you."

Jillian excused herself and left me alone with my gingerbread and fast disappearing cocoa. They had used real chocolate. I would happily submerge myself in a vat of this cocoa. And the gingerbread. Whoever made it could open a shop selling nothing but gingerbread and make a fortune. While she was gone, I rubbed the heel of one hand against my heart. What had that been? I've had crushes, but nothing ever so sudden or intense as that moment when I first saw Jillian.

Did I screw up my morphing? Is my human form broken? Should I try shifting again to see if I can fix whatever I did wrong?

I glanced around the room. If I shifted here, one of my antlers would go through the drywall. Accounting would probably not look kindly upon damage caused by an ill-advised and unnecessary morph. I mean, what could I tell them? I wasn't about to confess how intimately she'd affected me. I'd sound like a lovesick puppy. And I highly doubt that lovesick puppies are allowed to be on the team.

The Big Show is in three weeks. Do your job. I chided myself.

The door opened, and Jillian stuck her head in the door. "C'mon. We figured it out. I'm taking you to Little Italy."

I followed Jillian to the door. Jillian stopped at the closet to put on a coat, change her slippers for boots, wind a scarf around her neck and put on a beanie. I realized I was staring. "Sorry."

She shrugged. "Another new experience for you. Do you want to morph into winter clothes or do you want to borrow some?"

I glanced down. When I'd landed, I'd chosen one of the outfits I'd practiced—the red sweater and leggings, and I was wearing fluffy socks in lieu of other footwear. I considered then decided. "Borrow. Like you said, it's a new experience."

I had taken clothes on and off before—the ones I'd morphed into human form wearing—both for school and for fun. But this was different because these clothes weren't a part of me. They were foreign objects on my body. After next year, who knew if I'd ever help guide the sleigh again —I needed to savor these experiences. Sliding my arm through the silky interior lining of a woolen coat, then the scratchy wool at the cuffs. The solidness of a button, and the simple satisfaction that twisting it through the buttonhole could provide. The sole of the boot dragged on my foot when I lifted my foot to ensure I'd tied the laces right. The way Jillian's eyes crinkled at the edges as I fussily arranged my scarf. And the zing I felt when our hands touched passing the beanie cap between us.

We exited the building, and I turned to Jillian. "Are we going to walk, take the subway, or a taxi?"

"I'm not a reindeer, so it's a bit far for me to walk, but it's your choice."

"Can we take a taxi?"

"As you wish," Jillian said. "Do you want to flag it down?"

I felt glee as I walked confidently to the sidewalk, flung up my arm and shouted "TAXI!" Immediately one pulled over, and we climbed in. I noted the protective glass between us. The driver was a man in his late thirties or early forties. I wondered if he believed, and which list he belonged on. Only Santa, Mrs. Claus, and Rudolph could tell just by looking. The rest of us used the Naughty-or-Nice database.

"164 Mulberry in Little Italy," Jillian said. "The cross street is Grand Street."

"Do you have access to the N-o-N?" I asked Jillian, curious. I was certain that it wasn't against the rules to talk about things as long as we weren't specific. N-o-N was okay, Naughty-or-Nice database was not. I knew what the Pole had told me, but the Pole had also told me there was a strict dress code, so I wasn't certain.

She looked at me, and tilted her head as she thought. "Comet, you're in New York City. You could walk up to any person and tell them the truth about everything and they'd think you were having some mental health struggles. Or pulling a prank for YouTube. Don't stress about slipping up or using the wrong words. To answer your question, yes, but I'm the only one in the office. Do you want to know what's on your schedule for tomorrow?"

I nodded.

"You're meeting with the Eastern U.S. delegation in the morning. Comet already met with them and planned that part of the route, but you may want to make changes. They'll run you through it and then you can make the call. In terms of classic Christmas in New York, we can do window shopping on 5th Avenue, viewing the tree at Rockefeller Center, and/or *The Nutcracker* ballet."

"I was hoping we'd see the tree," I said. I'd seen the tree from the air, but despite its size, I hadn't gotten what anyone would call a good look.

"It's not Christmas in New York without the tree," Jillian said.

I bit my lip. I could have her reel off my schedule for the week like she was my secretary, but that felt cold and impersonal. She seemed kind. "Um, Jillian? I want to ask you for a favor. Would you be okay with calling me Claudia?"

"Of course! But only when we're out, you know? Otherwise I need to be more formal in the office. As you can see, we're not formal about much, but we use your title rather than your name," she said. She touched my hand, and I swear I felt the warmth through both sets of mittens. My mittens were a so-soft-I-want-to-keep-them green that matched the scarf and hat's color perfectly. Her set was a creamy white I would've been terrified of wearing for fear they'd be dirty in seconds.

She paid the driver, and we got out. I inhaled as I looked up and down the street. I couldn't identify the scents, but they made my mouth water as much as the gingerbread had. Perhaps—blasphemy—more.

Da Nico, said the red awning across the street. Stretching above it was a bright red fire escape in sharp contrast with the rest of the ones in sight, which were uniformly black. I followed Jillian inside, and we were seated at a table. I took off the outerwear and instantly felt more comfortable—while an interesting and worthwhile experience, I didn't think I'd be repeating this experiment—wearing someone else's outerwear made me overheated.

"You go ahead and order. I'll try anything," I said, when the waiter arrived, too overwhelmed by the menu.

"Let's start basic. Cheese pizza, please," Jillian said to the waiter. Then she turned back to me. "So, Claudia, I'm your P.A. for the duration of your year with us. Well, your month, as it were. Some of the team like to keep things professional and formal. Others prefer a more informal relationship. I don't want to pry, or to pressure you, but you should know I'm comfortable with either, with a preference for informality." She glanced away, hand brushing some hair behind her ear.

"I'd like to get to know you better." My motives might not have been pure, but I should at least get to know her so I could figure out if I had a real crush or if it was just hormones.

She smiled and I noticed, for the first time, her dimples appear.

I was a dead woman.

Dimples were my kryptonite.

Suddenly it felt as if I were wearing many layers of someone else's outerwear. Why was the room so hot? How had it changed so fast?

"So when exactly did you find out that you'd be taking

over this year?" Jillian gave me a smile. "It must have been quite a shock."

"This morning. I'm still not sure if I'm hallucinating."

Her eyes widened and her face went slack with shock. "This? *This* morning? Like not even twelve hours ago this morning?"

"Yes." She was right—it had been less than twelve hours. For me it was as if eons had passed.

"You are the bravest woman I've ever met." She shook her head.

If only you knew what a fraud I am.

I disagreed. "Any potential would jump at the opportunity. I was just lucky."

She raised an eyebrow at me as if to say *oh, really?* but let it go. "Your turn—ask a question."

"When did you leave home to live here?" I asked. How long would it take me to become conversant in and comfortable with the human world the way she was?

"Oh, I was born here," Jillian answered.

I knew some elves went their whole lives without coming to the Pole, but obviously I'd never met one before. Fascinated, I asked, "Have you visited?"

Our conversation was interrupted by the arrival of the pizza. I inhaled the intoxicating aroma. I could see the cheese gleaming against the deep red of the sauce and the golden crust. I picked up a piece and took a bite. The flavors exploded on my tongue and I closed my eyes in enjoyment.

"Well? What's the verdict?" Jillian raised her brows in question.

"This is amazing," I said. I took another greedy bite. "How do you not eat this all the time?"

She laughed. "There are many more foods to introduce you to. You'll have to tell me at the end of the week what you liked best. The great thing about you landing in New York means you can try a lot of different cuisines. And, of course, you have the six months after Christmas to explore anywhere in the world and try more food."

I picked up my second slice. "Sorry, we got derailed—have you ever visited home?"

"I trained there for a little over a year when I was promoted to Personal Assistant. It was a whole other way of life, and I'll admit I never quite felt like I fit in. But I might be moving there, if... I mean, probably not, though. Rudolph's P.A. is retiring, and they've asked the eight regional P.A.'s to put in an application. One in eight aren't the best odds, though. Still, the challenge of looking at the worldwide route? I know I could kill it."

"You'd have to move to the Pole?"

Please move to the Pole!

"If I get the job, but like I said, the odds are low. I'd really miss my family. Part of me wonders if I could handle living at the Pole six months or more a year. After living at the Pole I will say that I get why Zen talks about how it's always Christmas dialed up to an aggressive ten there."

"She said fourteen to me." I laughed.

"The closer it gets to Christmas the more pressure she's under. There are so many hi-tech elements to Christmas these days, and the buck stops with her. So in June we all enjoy Christmas at an eight, then it's a ten by September, and so on, higher and higher until you're back from the Big Show."

I nodded. "Lots of pressure to be a Personal Assistant, though, too. Especially Rudolph's."

"True. But I didn't get activated this morning," she replied with another flash of those distracting dimples.

We finished up, and Jillian took me to 5th Avenue where we hiked north past department stores with magical windows. Here a child could turn a steering wheel outside the window and the truck in the window turned in response. There a store's façade had been turned into a castle. And there was a window with what looked like a magic mirror in it along with a bunch of other fairy-tale themed windows.

Every so often our hands would brush, and I wished I was brave enough to ask if she liked me. If she wanted to hold hands. If she wanted to kiss me. It was too fast to feel that, wasn't it?

"We should head back, though," she said.

"Can we—" I yawned, distorting the word "—take a cab back? I'm feeling tired."

"Of course," she said, walked to the street and hailed a cab for us.

In the cab I felt my eyelids grow leaden, and the last thing I remembered was my head falling onto Jillian's shoulder. After what seemed like only seconds, we were back uptown and Jillian was rousing me.

"C'mon sleepyhead. Let's get you upstairs," she said, leaning in to offer me a hand out of the cab.

Yawning and rubbing my eyes, I followed her through the lobby—the tree there was done up in silver and gold. The elves' work was exquisite—the spacing and symmetry of design would have appealed to me even more if I hadn't wanted to just lie down on the floor and sleep. I sagged against the wall of the elevator.

"I think your day is catching up to you. Even with Christmas Magic it's been a long one. But don't worry, your energy is also ramping up. In a week you'll still be wide awake, in two weeks you'll be ready to go out dancing all night, and in three you'll be flying around the world. I'm told you will sleep for twenty-four or so hours after the flight, but that during the flight you feel completely aware and awake," Jillian reassured me. "Do you want me to show you to the bedroom or the stall? They're connected, so it's up to you."

"The stall," I said, ready to morph.

It was full of fresh hay and there was a lovely blanket that Jillian offered to lay over me. Gratefully, I morphed, sank to the ground, and was asleep before I felt the blanket touch me.

Chapter Three

The first rays of sunlight streaming into my stall woke me. Yawning, I struggled to my feet, then morphed into human form. I walked through the reindeer-sized doorway into a human bedroom. There was what seemed like an unnecessarily large bed covered in sumptuous green bedding. A birch nightstand sat on either side of the bed, and on top of each nightstand was a gold lamp. I decided to check out the bathroom. It was floor to ceiling white marble with veins of gold twining throughout. I caught my breath. There was a luxurious walk-in shower and a separate whirlpool tub.

I watched my reflection in the gold mirror above the sink. I didn't want to embarrass myself. The elves here had hair in every color of the rainbow. Should I try that? I morphed my hair turquoise, magenta, green, and silver, but it didn't feel like me, somehow. I shook my head and went back to my standard brown. For clothing, I'd chosen a green shirt inspired by the duvet color, and black slacks.

Today was my first day on the job for real. Crossing my fingers, I whispered "pleasepleaseplease let this go well."

Elves in various degrees of wakefulness were drinking from mugs in the kitchen.

"Morning. Coffee, Comet?" One of the more awake elves asked.

Stifling another yawn, I nodded, and in moments had a welcome, hot cup of candy cane coffee in my hands.

"Heads up, everyone. Jillian said we're meeting in twenty. Comet, you should meet her in her office whenever you're ready."

"I'm ready now," I said, carrying my mug. We walked to Jillian's office, where she was drinking her own coffee.

"Good morning, Comet." She picked up a tablet with her free hand. "So, this morning we're getting right into planning the route. We're meeting with the Eastern U.S. delegation first since Wendy was going to be taking control of the route in Rio, Brazil and she—now, you—would lead the Eastern North America route from Rio to where you hand off to Cupid. I'm a little unclear where that hand-off is happening, though. The U.S. delegation has your data on who we're making in-person deliveries to, and we can look at how this year's flight path might change from last year."

"I have the notes from Cupid, who did this region last year. Comet sent them to me, along with her notes and tentative flight path. She and Cupid had been debating if they wanted to hand off in Louisiana or the Northern Territories of Canada."

"Great. If you don't mind, follow me." Jillian led me to a meeting room down the hall. Four elves sat around the table—representatives from the U.S. who would help me tweak the route. I'd meet with representatives from Eastern Canada in a few days.

"Comet, this is Joao, Marc, Alicia, and Lena. Everyone, this is Comet."

We all shook hands and got down to business. Miami, Florida was the first city we looked at. There were two hundred addresses in the city center alone, with a number of differences from last year. Joao used one of Zen's inventions to project an interactive 3-D map of Miami above the table, so we could debate approaches.

Geena appeared in the doorway and knocked. "Sorry to bother you guys, but there's a call from Rudolph for Comet."

Have I done something wrong already?

"You can take it in my office for some privacy if you want," Jillian offered.

"She said she needs both of you," Geena said.

"That's strange," Jillian murmured. "If everyone can excuse us?"

What on earth could I have done to merit Rudolph's attention?

Jillian moved briskly to the sofa in her office and patted the spot next to her. "Comet, if you come sit next to me, we can take the call on my tablet."

Rudolph's human face came onscreen. "Listen up. We have a crisis on our hands. For some reason, we're suddenly losing believers in cities all around the world. Not just any believers—top-of-the-Nice-list believers. This is unprecedented. You two will need to deal with the newly non-believing. Please try to figure out what's happening as soon as you can. I've had Zen add a feature to the N-o-N database so you can track the people you need to find in real time."

Jillian frowned. "What about the delegations that are here to help Comet plan her route?"

"Transport them to me. I'm going to be planning the world-wide route from the Pole with all of the delegations so we can have the rest of you focus on the nonbelievers."

I was confused as to how I could possibly be of any

help. I was so new here, I felt like I had no idea what direction I was even going in. "Rudolph, are you sure you want me on this? I mean, it's only my first time in the human world, and I—"

"Comet, are you telling me you can't do your job?" Rudolph said sharply.

"No," I said quickly.

"There's at least one city in every region having a crisis of belief. All the other reindeer are busy in their own regions and cities. Wendy is too pregnant, although you have permission to rope her in remotely if you want. But really, you and Jillian are in charge of finding out what's happening in New York."

With that, Rudolph's image winked out. The only sound in the room was my uneven breathing. I turned and looked at Jillian.

"I can't do this."

"Sure you can," she assured me. "It's—"

"No, no, I can't." My lungs grew leaden while my heartbeat grew erratic and panicky.

"Don't worry. We'll do it together." Our gazes locked when her hand touched my shoulder. For a moment it was just her and me, and nothing else existed.

I sucked in a shaky breath. "I just…it's so much."

Suddenly I was wrapped in a hug. My head fell on her shoulder and I buried my face in the curve of her neck. She smelled like her coffee, and something else… A lighter, almost citrus scent beneath that—maybe her shampoo or a lotion.

"What if I screw up?" My words were a whisper against her skin.

She stroked my back and made comforting sounds. "I think I'd be scared of the same thing," she said. "But you haven't failed. We haven't even tried yet."

"You're right."

"I'm going to send off everyone and get them to Rudolph. Do you want to come with me, or start in your office?"

"I want to get to work," I said.

I had been assigned the office next to hers. It was time to examine the N-o-N database. Just how bad was it?

Twenty top believers had just stopped cold yesterday. Three weeks before Christmas was the time we usually *added* believers, not lost them—and we certainly didn't lose people from the top of the Nice list. The overwhelming majority of those who'd lost faith were children between the ages of five and thirteen, and the six adults were women around my age. What was up with that? They lived all over the place—one little boy was from Florida, but was staying in New York, so it wasn't something like a specific address or a shared school that tied the believers together.

I knew we had to track them down. Zen's new feature allowed me to see where a person was in real time. I picked up my phone, which was in human mode—no magic, no access to the N-o-N, none of that. I used a touch of Christmas magic and it changed to Pole mode with all the North Pole icons so I could see the N-o-N. There was a note from Zen the first time I opened it. It said *This is a temporary feature on this app because it's creepy AF to be stalking people like this.* I gave a little snort of amusement. She wasn't wrong.

Jillian believed I could do this, so I was going to do it. Or so I told the pressure building between my shoulder blades. A five-minute guided meditation was exactly what I needed, so I took a moment and put in my earbuds. As I followed the instructions, I felt things loosen in my torso and my breathing evened out.

When I opened my eyes, I screamed. Jillian jumped and gave a little shriek herself.

"I didn't mean to scare you! I just didn't want to interrupt!" Jillian gasped.

"Oh, man, I'm sorry. I just didn't expect to, y'know, find you there," I said.

"I wanted to let you know the American and Canadian delegations passed on good wishes for this year's flight and for our side mission," Jillian said. "So how do you want to go about this?"

"I think we should try to talk to someone our own age first. Maybe split the list—we each take three?" I said.

Jillian agreed. "I don't think we need to rope in any of the New York elves until we get an idea of what these new non-believers have to say."

She nodded, and we split it up. She gave me an ID and credit card for *Claudia Comet*, some cash, and an MTA card so I could get around more easily. Having to keep my phone in Pole mode made me antsy, but I had no other choice while I was searching out non-believers. I clutched it, though, determined not to lose it or to let a human see.

As I entered the subway. I was deeply grateful for my Christmas magic. I couldn't get lost, which was fortunate, given how intricate and confusing the subway map might look to someone without an innate GPS.

The first person on my list was a woman named Michaela Danvers. I clicked on the icon and found her in a bar in Soho. I was lucky Jillian had thought of ID because I was carded at the door. I took a seat on a stool, looking for Michaela.

"Can I get you something?" a bartender approached me. It was her.

Great, I'd found her. Now what?

Comet's First Christmas

"Can I have—" *What do I order? I'll get it wrong and then I'll get this whole assignment wrong.* "—a Coke?"

She nodded and got it for me. The bar was quiet, so she was nearby, without hovering over me or the other patrons. I enjoyed the fizz of the bubbles and the sugary sweetness of the Coke, but I was focused on watching Michaela surreptitiously. Before yesterday, she'd asked for and was going to get a new laptop to replace the one that was falling to pieces so she could finish her book. Had she stopped believing in her writing? No, that wouldn't explain it.

"So, what brings you here today? Taking a break from shopping?" Michaela asked me.

"Oh, man, I haven't even started," I lied. "How about you?"

Michaela smiled. "I decided I'm skipping gifts this year."

Raising an eyebrow, I asked. "Really? Why, if you don't mind my asking?"

"Because it's a ton of pressure to get the right gift and if you get a bad one it somehow says something about your relationship with that person, right? It's as bad as Valentine's Day!"

"Don't you think there's kind of a huge difference between Christmas and Valentine's Day?"

"No, seriously, I met this guy last night and he convinced me. It's so freeing to say screw Christmas. If you haven't started yet, why bother?" Michaela said, pouring me another drink.

So who was this guy and why had his opinion changed her mind so abruptly?

"I think my family would be really disappointed in me if I suddenly stopped participating in Christmas," I replied carefully. "Won't your family care?"

She shrugged. "I'm not going home this Christmas. I told the boss I'd work."

"I can't imagine not wanting to celebrate Christmas. Do you have a favorite tradition?" If I could convince her to believe again, it would prove that I deserved to be on the team, and that I can do my job.

"I thought so, too, just a few days ago. But it's all a marketing scam. Santa, trees, all that jazz—all to make money," she shrugged.

Another bartender came in. He tapped Michaela on the shoulder. "You're free."

"Well, I'm off. Good luck with the shopping," Michaela said and walked away.

That didn't go well.

The next former believer was a woman named Reyna Junto, who worked in a giant skyscraper in midtown I couldn't get into. I could turn invisible, but how would I explain myself once I found her? I decided to circle back to her.

I hiked uptown. Unlike humans or elves, this amount of walking was nothing to me, thanks to reindeer endurance and my magic. Coach Prancer would be proud of me doing all this walking in human form. I tried to walk at a similar pace as the native New Yorkers, who zipped through the pedestrian traffic with a skill that seemed almost as magical as my own talents. Did Jillian walk like this when she was on her own? She was as much a New Yorker as these people were.

The final person on my list was Samantha Reston at the David H. Koch theater. I looked up at the columned building and wondered how I was going to get to her. Then I saw the huge banners for *The Nutcracker*. Hadn't Jillian mentioned something about this ballet? That there were tickets? I called Jillian.

"Hey, Claudia. I'm sorry, I'm having the worst luck," Jillian said when she picked up. "I've talked to two of the women, and the only thing they have in common is that they talked to some guy in a bar yesterday. But not even the same bar. I didn't manage to get a description of the guy, though."

I frowned. "I've only talked to one of the three women on my list, but it was the same story. There must be thousands of bars in this city, though. There aren't enough elves to stake out every bar in Manhattan."

"No. We can't do that, and even if we could, how would we interrogate every man that entered to ask if they've been ruining Christmas for believers?"

"The last woman on my list works in the building where *Nutcracker* is playing. Did you say we had tickets? Do you think we could maybe find her after a show?" I asked.

"Good idea. Yes, we have tickets for tonight. I was going to give them away if we were going to be working, but let's use them and see what we can find out," Jillian agreed.

I went back to Reyna's work and staked it out. To make the eight o'clock curtain I needed to leave by seven-thirty, but I had plenty of time to wait. By the time six rolled around, my patience paid off. I saw Reyna leaving her office with a rolling bag.

I'd decided on my approach during lunch. I had asked for a clipboard, a pen, and a petition with a number of signatures on it. The elves had delivered it within the hour of my requesting it.

"Hi! Excuse me?" I approached Reyna. "I'm trying to petition the city to have a craft fair for children. The kids make and sell the crafts, then the money can be used for holiday activities from class parties to seeing the Christmas Spectacular."

"If you're going to petition the city, there are a lot of better causes. More money for teachers, better subway maintenance, more social workers—why Christmas?" she asked. She hadn't agreed, but she didn't seem angry.

I had only a muddy understanding, at best, of what a social worker even was. I decided to let it go and barrel on.

"Because it's a magical time of the year? Especially for kids. The trees, caroling, Santa? Don't you think Christmas is magic?"

She shrugged. "I used to."

"Why no more?"

She looked at me. "Don't you think we're a little old for Santa Claus?"

Shaking my head, I replied with sincerity. "No. I don't. I believe in Santa. I leave out carrots for the reindeer, and they're always gone. Aren't they gone for you?"

Carrots helped fuel the way across the US, which was part of the last zones in the world to be flown during the Big Show. Other countries had other traditions, but the carrots were a favored part of the flight.

She bit her lip. "I thought they were, but I must have put them away. I mean, Santa slipping down my fire escape to put new boots in my apartment? Sounds like I had too much to drink."

"I'm hoping to get some jewelry," I said. "A special necklace I've wanted a long time."

Not the most common description of a reindeer's harness, but close enough.

"Why do you believe?" she asked.

"I'm pretty sure I saw Santa once. When I was a kid."

I saw him five days ago and his beard is coming in nicely.

"Based on a dream you had as a kid you still believe? Just because I had a nightmare about Krampus once doesn't mean I think *he* is real."

Krampus used to be Santa's opposite—the punisher of bad children. I certainly wouldn't want a demon beating me with birch branches. But as society changed, his mythos changed, and he was forced to retire a little over a hundred years ago because of declining belief.

"And the gifts that still come. Isn't there always an unlabeled gift? And it's always something you wanted?" I pushed.

Her face clouded, then cleared. "I'll sign."

Once she had scribbled her name on the petition, she glanced at her watch and blanched. "I have to go. Good luck. Thanks for reminding me of why I always loved this holiday. Why should some dude in a bar change something that's made me happy? Screw him."

"A guy in a bar?" I tried desperately. "Sounds like someone I'd want to avoid."

"It was Duke's on Second Avenue. I forget the guy's name. Our age. Brown hair. Kinda cute in a generic way. But if he starts talking about the commercialization of Christmas, run!" She said the last with a laugh. "I don't know if he could convert you—you seem like a hardcore believer. Merry Christmas!"

"Merry Christmas!"

I glanced at my phone. I'd repaired her belief in Christmas! I didn't completely suck at my new job!

Jillian and I met at the theater, and we made our way to our seats. My phone wasn't more helpful. I just knew she was somewhere backstage, but that meant she could be anything from a stage hand to a dancer to a costumer to any one of probably a hundred or so jobs.

Frustrated, I began paging through my program. Then I stopped. Samantha Reston was dancing the role of the Sugar Plum Fairy. I nudged Jillian and indicated my program.

"Well that makes it hard for us to get to her," Jillian murmured in my ear. Her breath was warm on my ear, and gooseflesh broke out on my arms. I was deeply grateful that they were covered by my jacket. "But at least we get to enjoy the show?"

"True," I replied.

I settled in and let the music wash over me. The small children dancing in the party scene and in the mice battle were adorable, and I couldn't help but grin at their performances. I'd read that the kids were all students at the School of American Ballet. They must be so excited to have a chance to perform like this. I wondered if any of the kids onstage were newly non-believers, or if it was just Samantha.

I gasped when the tree grew. *The Nutcracker* was a popular ballet at the Pole, so I'd known it was coming, but it was just so magical. Up, up, up it went until I felt like I, too, had shrunk to fit beneath it.

"It's one of the best *Nutcracker* trees," Jillian's voice whispered into my ear. "I'm so glad you like it."

During intermission Jillian went to make a call. I gave into impulse and went to the theater's merchandise stall. I couldn't resist buying a poster for myself, an ornament for Wendy, and, on impulse, a shirt for Jillian as a thank you for bringing me. And for everything. As a thank you. Not as a please-date-me gift. A thank you.

I leaned forward when Samantha took the stage in the second act. She moved like an angel. Every movement of her body was precise and lyrical at the same time. She danced like she *was* the Sugar Plum Fairy. When thunderous applause began after she'd struck her last pose, I noticed she jumped a little. Just like I'd jumped when Jillian had been there this morning after my meditation—a start at coming back to the real world from wherever I'd been in my head. Where did Samantha go went when she danced?

After the show, they announced that some of the dancers would be in the lobby to take photos as long as you donated to their fund to give scholarships to talented young dancers. Jillian and I got in line to meet Samantha. We made sure we were last in line, which we hoped would give us a chance to talk to her.

"Thank you for such an amazing performance!" Jillian greeted Samantha when it was finally our turn.

"Thank you!" she said. "Whose phone should we use for the photograph?"

I quickly handed my phone—in *human* mode—to the person taking the photos.

"You look like someone who really believes in Christmas magic," I opened. Jillian's eyes widened, but she didn't step in.

Samantha laughed. "I get that a lot. But I think I'm just hitting a wall this year. I mean someone tried to talk me out of this role last night. I mean, over my dead body. I worked for my whole life for this role. But they made good points about Santa. I mean, we're all a little old for Santa, right?"

Jillian and I replied in unison. "No."

"Is it too late to get our picture?" A family with a young boy was standing there.

"No," said Samantha. "Nice meeting you ladies. You make a cute couple!"

I was torn between protesting that we weren't together and asking her if she really, really meant it.

"Thanks," Jillian responded smoothly. "C'mon, Claudia. Don't forget your phone."

The photographer handed it back to me. I glanced

through the photos, and realized that Samantha was right. Jillian and I looked really pretty together.

Yes, well, she's probably not into you in that way.

"Send me copies of the photos?" Jillian asked as we walked back to the New York HQ.

"Of course," I said, forwarding the photos to her phone.

"She's right. We do look cute together," Jillian looked at her phone, swiping through all three. "So what's our next move?"

We look cute together? What does that mean? Just that we look cute together or we look cute together?

"Well, I wonder if bar guy is the same person who talked the kids into not believing. It would be difficult, don't you think? We'll need a different tactic to talk to kids. No parent is going to react well to a random stranger approaching their kid and I can't pass for a child. I can sort of shift to the size of a teenager, but I can't mimic the way a child moves their body or know what kids like and all that. I'm going to need to think."

At the door to my stall, I turned to Jillian and stammered. "I— I got—"

Jillian raised an eyebrow.

No! You will look like a stupid lovesick puppy. What if she laughs at you?

"Sorry, never mind. Good night, Jillian."

"Good night, Claudia."

Jillian gave me an easy hug. "Don't worry. We'll figure something out."

I nodded and watched her walk away. Shaking my head, I put my bag in the closet of the human room. I called Wendy for advice but there was no answer. I left a message and decided to try again tomorrow.

Chapter Four

From: Jillian
To: Claudia
Subject: Idea for approaching kids

> I think I have a solution to our how-do-we-approach-the-children problem. I have a little sister named Lee. She's nine, and could easily approach children.
> Let's talk about it when I get in tomorrow morning.

Using an elf child was just plain risky, wasn't it? Maybe I could morph into a kid-sized human after all, if I tried hard enough? I stood and tried to morph to look like a child. What I'd told Jillian still held true. My height barely changed, and my features still looked too mature. Frustrated, I let my appearance morph back to my human standard. I certainly couldn't pass for a child, and neither could Jillian.

Jillian's sister was nine. She couldn't possibly take this all seriously, could she? Could she protect the Pole?

My computer started chiming. It was Wendy, who I could see reclined in a chair with pillows tucked in all around her. She held a steaming mug in her hands.

"Claudia! How are things?"

I have a huge crush on my P.A. and I'm terrified of letting everyone down.

"They could be going better," I said, rubbing my temples.

"I'm sure. I'm so sorry I'm not there to handle this. How can I help?" She took a sip and grimaced. "This prenatal tea is disgusting."

"And you'll drink it three times a day the way the doctor told you to," came a voice from off-screen.

Wendy rolled her eyes. "Yes, oh beloved wife. Anyway," she said, returning her attention to me "what have you found out so far?"

I shared about yesterday's detective work and what we'd learned. "Today, though, we want to start focusing on the kids. How would you talk to children if you were me?"

Wendy turned thoughtful. "I'd see if any of them were in Times Square. We must own or have access to one of the hokey elf costumes. Parents might go for photos with one of Santa's elves. Then I could talk to the children when they came over. But a lot has to go right in that scenario and I'd be looking for better solutions. I know everyone is struggling with the question of how to reach out to the children. Christmas magic can do a lot, but it can't be used to manipulate humans into letting strangers talk to their kids."

"Jillian suggested we enlist her little sister to help us. But she's only nine," I said. "Isn't that dangerous? What if she talks about things she shouldn't?"

Comet's First Christmas

I'd met elf children at the Pole. They were like any other kid I'd seen in media. They went to school. They played games. They didn't help out with high-stakes missions.

"Actually, that's potentially a great option, with the right kid. If it works, Rudolph will count that in Jillian's favor. I hear competition for the assistant job is intense." Wendy nodded as if mulling the idea over in her head.

"Isn't nine a little young to get involved though?" I asked skeptically.

"Not necessarily. Elf children raised in the human world aren't like elf children here at the Pole—they're more mature and better understand the need for absolutely secrecy." Wendy advised. "I'd reach out to Cupid—she had the region last year. She's probably met Jillian's little sister. Besides, you're asking for help on one thing, not signing her up for her apprenticeship or a full-time private investigator gig."

"Okay. I'll call Cupid and see what she says." I nodded.

"Unless Cupid says Jillian's sister is a train wreck, I'd consider using her." She sipped from her mug and wrinkled her nose. "Anyway, tell me about your first time away from the Pole. Have you tasted any human food yet?"

I grinned. "Cheese pizza. Now I understand why pizza is so popular! What was your first human food?"

"My first region was Western North America. Nico had me meet him in Austin, Texas, and took me to a working lunch with barbecue brisket. Man, now I want brisket. Human food is always a highlight of joining the team. I mean flying is cool and all, but have you ever had a freshly baked fudgy brownie?" She winked at me when I burst into laughter. "With the non-believer stuff, did you get a chance to use my tickets to the ballet last night or did you have to skip it?"

I shared about the ballet and meeting Samantha. Wendy seemed glad I'd enjoyed the show, but a little wistful she'd missed out. We talked for several minutes more before she needed to leave for a doctor's appointment.

I found Cupid's contact pre-programmed into my phone along with numbers for the whole team and—oh my—Santa and Mrs. Claus. There were two numbers I didn't think I'd ever have the nerve to use.

I pressed the button to call Cupid, and she picked up almost immediately. She wore black-rimmed glasses I knew for a fact she didn't need—all reindeer have perfect vision —and her blonde hair was in a bun at the nape of her neck. If I remembered right, she was a college professor in the spring semester. Was this her professor look or did she exude a bit of the sexy librarian vibe all the time?

"Hi, new girl, how can I help you? Have you learned anything?" Cupid asked with a kind smile.

"I talked to the adult non-believing yesterday. The only common thread was some grinch at a bar, but when we got bar names from three of them, they were different bars."

"I started with adults, too, and I'm hearing the same story. So are Prancer and Dasher. Zen is frustrated because unlike the rest of us, Zen has *two* cities with sharply declining believers and she's bouncing between Singapore and Hong Kong like a pinball. Dancer talked to a child yesterday and all they could say was that a mean adult talked to them on the bus. What are we supposed to do with that? Close down all the bars and buses? Vix can find her non-believers—easy enough in Australia and New Zealand. But when she made her car break down near one of their homes, the parents helped but she never got a chance to have a private conversation with the kids, and another house had vicious dogs. She's going to focus on adults while she regroups. Donner decided to play imaginary friend—turn invisible and talk to children—but I think it will backfire on her, and she admits she's freaked out several kids. She heard about a mean Santa, so she's going to try to track him down. That's the only other lead. A mean Santa and a grinch in bars or on busses talking people out of believing in Santa isn't much to go on."

I wasn't sure whether to be relieved that the other reindeer weren't doing miles better than I was, because I sucked, or worried because they weren't, and that left us still pretty clueless as to why people were falling off the believers list. Maybe my best wasn't terrible, but it wasn't good enough either. There was just under three weeks until Christmas. How many hundreds of believers would we lose by then—or worse, how many thousands?

"Cupid, I was partially calling you to ask you about Jillian's little sister. Jillian suggested enlisting her to help us talk to the kids. Since you had the region last year, Wendy thought you might have some thoughts. You've met her, right?" I twirled a pen between my fingers.

"Yes, her name is Jubilee, but she goes by Lee. She's all about the Pole and helping the team. It made her so happy that I kept finding her tiny errands last year. I started with things like can you get me some coffee—little things I could easily do myself. But she was always punctual, always ready to help, waited patiently when I didn't have anything for her to do—just read a book—that I decided to give her bigger errands. She started to go to the corner bodega to get my favorite sandwich—I'll email the deets for you to try, if you want—and kept me in gum. When that went well, I let her sit in on a few logistics meetings—I was sure it would bore her—but instead she sat quietly until someone needed something and then she'd deal with it. So basically she was our errand girl—but she was trustworthy enough at eight to do that—yes, even to run to the corner bodega on her own!

"I can only imagine how she'll feel to be singled out to help you like this. You can trust her not to divulge that she's an elf or that you're a reindeer or any of that. She's grown up in New York, so she's savvy in a way you're not used to children being. She knows how to navigate the subway—she doesn't ride without an adult, but she can tell you how to get from point a to b on the subway with only a map. She even has playdates with human kids. It's not the worst idea I've heard. Maybe I should see if there's an elf kid in my region I can borrow like that. Let us know if it works, because if it does, we all might want to adopt that approach," Cupid said.

"I will, I promise," I said.

"Good luck, new girl."

About fifteen minutes after my call ended, Jillian knocked on my open office door. "Is now a good time?" At my nod, she invited her sister into the room. Even if I hadn't known they were sisters, it was clear as day. "Lee, this is Comet. Comet, this is my sister, Lee."

I gave a little wave. "Hi, Lee."

"It's really nice to meet you, Comet. Jilly said you might need my help?" Her eyes were so hopeful I could feel my heart warming toward the young elf immediately.

"That's right. I think you can do something none of the rest of us can do."

"Because there are kids, right? I can talk to the kids."

I glanced at Jillian. "And your mom will be okay with it?"

Nodding, Jillian said, "Anything for the Pole."

"Anything for the Pole," Lee echoed.

"You're sure that you can talk to human kids without revealing anything about us?"

She sighed and rolled her eyes a bit—a clear indication she thought that was a stupid question. I almost cracked up laughing, but managed to keep a straight face. I didn't want to offend her or Jillian.

"Of *course*. I have human friends I see at the playground every day," Lee said indignantly. "I watch the same YouTubers. I've never, and would never, tell them about the Pole."

Well, Wendy and Cupid were right; Lee wasn't like any child I'd met at the Pole. She was a dual-cultured elf who knew and understood our ways, but who also understood the humans well. I glanced up—just like her older sister. Was having this kind of dual-culture part of what made Jillian such a good P.A.? Would it help or hurt her chances at being selected as Rudolph's next P.A.? I pushed down a bit of envy—I could be on the team for twenty years and still not be as proficient in human culture as she was and her sister was becoming.

"I'm sorry. I didn't mean to hurt your feelings. I'd definitely like you to help us today, if you still want to," I said.

Lee jumped up and down, and I found myself smiling. She might be more mature than most of the Pole kids, but she was still a kid. She went downstairs to her apartment to get ready for her day out with us. Jillian and I looked at the kids' data and found a number clustered along a stretch of Fifth Avenue and at Rockefeller Center.

"Guess we're going ice skating," Jillian said.

She got dressed for the chilly weather while I morphed into winter clothes, although I did borrow the super soft mittens from two nights ago. We picked up Lee on the tenth floor, then took the subway and walked to Rockefeller Center. On the walk there, I confirmed that there were kids we needed to talk to who were ice skating or next to the ice skaters. It was slow going to click through every profile. I used my Christmas magic to ensure I didn't walk into anyone, but I kept my head bent over my phone.

"Claudia," Jillian said.

I looked at her quizzically. Amused, she gestured ahead of us.

"Don't you love it?" Lee squealed, pointing.

I'd been so absorbed in my task that I'd completely missed where we were. I looked up and saw the tree with Rockefeller Center perfectly framed behind it.

"Oh. It's wonderful," I breathed.

There was an astoundingly beautiful Norway spruce, easily eighty, maybe eighty-five feet tall. It was covered in ornaments and large colorful bulbs. I had to crane my neck to see the massive star atop it. I inhaled happily, that comforting scent of home giving me a pang of homesickness. It loomed over a large ice-skating rink down a big set of stairs.

"Here. These children are here, Lee. Can you try to find one of them?" I offered my phone to Lee to memorize the names and faces. "Review for me what you're going to do when you find them."

"I'll talk about other stuff and then Christmas. Then bring up Santa," Lee said with a bright smile. She curled her body around my phone, understanding it was vulnerable to exposing Christmas magic while in Pole mode. Frowning, she stared at each picture for a few moments, nodded to herself, and then flicked to the next picture. When finished, she gave me my phone back with a solemn nod, this time to me.

The three of us went to the skate rental and got our skates. We were lucky that there was a lull and not a huge line, as Jillian had been worried about. Hopefully that luck would hold.

The skates were shockingly heavy but I wasn't worried.

"Have you skated in human form?" Jillian asked, watching me lace them up.

"Of course! I love it," I replied, "and unlike here, I can ice skate year-round. I can't wait to get on the ice."

"You should know that you guys usually struggle at first." She tried to caution me.

"I'm sure I'll be fine." I dismissed her concern.

Once on the ice, Lee took off like a shot. I saw her weaving in and out of the other skaters as she looked for the right humans. Jillian stepped on the ice and skated backwards, her arm out to me. I confidently stepped on the ice and immediately grabbed Jillian.

"Every single time," she said with a laugh.

"What?"

"You guys," she said with a dimpled smile. "None of you can ice skate right off. The weight of the skates throws you off. Don't worry, though, it's temporary, and even reindeer as experienced as Zen have issues every year because you forget to adjust for the weight of the skate. You'll be skating in no time, though. Just take a turn around the ice with me a few times and then you'll get it. Until then, I've got you."

I had learned how to skate in human form after I'd learned to morph, so I'd always created my skates the way I created my boots or anything else I wore on my feet. But that was not an option out in full view of all these humans. I'd just have to get used to these clumsy, weighty skates.

She offered her hand to me. We skated hand in hand as I stumbled and slipped and jerked my body around the ice. Just as she promised, though, my body slowly adapted to the skates, and I found the right rhythm. By our third turn around the ice, I no longer needed Jillian to stay upright and it finally registered that I was holding hands with her.

I kept an eye on Lee, who was deep in discussion with a

child—April Jasper, age nine, top percentage of the Nice list for three years running—as they circled the rink.

I felt guilty for holding onto Jillian once I was steady on the ice, even as I was reluctant to give up custody of her hand. "I think I'm solid."

"It's your first time. You can hold on—I don't mind," she said in a tone of voice I couldn't decipher. Did she want to hold hands with me? Or was she just doing her job? It was the same tone of voice she'd used last night when she'd seen our pictures and agreed we looked cute together.

I left my hand in hers, and even though I knew it was a fantasy, I let myself pretend for a moment that we were here on a date.

"Are you Lee's moms?" a voice came from behind us.

"I'm her sister," Jillian said.

"She seems like a love. April and she are getting along like a house on fire. Can I get a number? Maybe we can do a playdate?" the woman said. She pulled out her phone and skated with us as Jillian recited what I assumed was her mother's cell phone number.

When April's mom had left, I looked at Jillian with a wink. "A couple yesterday, moms today. Gosh we're moving fast." Then my eyes widened in horror. I'd never been good at flirting, and, more to the point, it was inappropriate for me to flirt with her!

She smirked at me. "Are you saying I shouldn't have put a deposit on a house in Jersey with a yard and a dog?"

The sudden rockslide in my chest paused and receded. She'd flirted back. *What did that mean?* Was I brave enough to keep it up?

I smirked back. "I'm a cat person."

She laughed. "Of course you are."

The Pole didn't have a vermin problem often, but we kept cats around people's homes and the barn just in case. As far as I could tell it was both effective at keeping creatures away and an excuse to have a housecat to dote upon. I didn't have a cat (yet), but I still went to my mom's house to play with Lady, her sleek, black cat. And I sometimes slipped little morsels of salmon to my neighbor's cat, Tybalt.

I should really get a cat.

A little later Lee came over to us. "I have some information, but do you want me to find another kid first?"

"Yes, let me look to see who is here." April had left with her parents to get food. I searched my phone and found one child at the rink—Dani Trevalo, age eight, first year on the top of the Nice list.

Lee took off again.

Jillian and I took a break from skating and sat on a bench, watching Lee do her thing. Looking up above the rink, I saw a couple by the tree that looked like—I elbowed Jillian and pointed— Yes, there was a proposal! A successful one, based on the cheers of the onlookers.

"Looks like they're making their own Christmas magic." She sighed with pleasure.

I murmured my agreement, while drowning hopelessly in my crush.

"I'm guessing they don't prepare you for this sort of thing in school." Jillian turned to face me.

I frowned. "Proposals?"

She laughed. "No, I meant chasing down bad dudes in bars talking people out of believing."

"Yeah, no training on that." I glanced over to where Lee was talking to Dani. "You know, both Wendy and Cupid thought your idea was so good that if we have success, all the reindeer should try it. That Rudolph would count it toward your application to be his P.A. I hope I can help you look good."

Jillian blushed a pretty pink. "Thanks. I wasn't thinking of Rudolph when I suggested it, but I guess it makes sense that how we work with our reindeer and address this believer crisis will influence her decision. Wow, like we needed more pressure." Then she shook her head. "Let's just focus on the job—tracking down the criminal behind this scheme."

I opened my mouth to reply, but Lee clomped over to us, and she dropped down on Jillian's far side. "Okay, guys, I got the scoop—I talked to a bunch of kids, not just April and Dani. Consensus is that the Santa at the Bryant Park Christmas Fair and the Santa at Macy's are the bad ones. April and Dani both said that when the Santa started telling them they were bad, they got angry. Can you believe he told them that they were stupid for thinking they were good? Then he told them something specific they'd done wrong that counted for the Naughty list. April was warning the rest of us not to let our parents take us to Macy's. This boy named Henry was the first person to tell me about Bryant Park, but he said that the Santa was liar, and he still believed. When I asked if April and Dani believed, both of them said not anymore, and their presents can be from their parents. It was so sad."

"If the Santas are able to tell kids something specific that the kids have done that puts them on the Naughty list, it means they have to have something like our Pole phone," I said. "I should tell Zen. Maybe she'll be able to track it somehow."

After taking a car back to the headquarters, we dropped Lee off. When I told her how proud everyone at the Pole would be of her, she glowed with pleasure. She made me promise to ping her if we needed more help with kids.

Once upstairs in my office, Jillian and I called Zen.

"What's up Ki—Comet?" Zen asked, cutting herself off before she called me "Kid Comet" in front of Jillian.

I debriefed Zen, and as I did so, Zen started cursing in a guttural language I didn't understand.

I felt tension form over my chest like a breastplate. Had I done the right thing? Should we have spent the rest of the day tracking down kids? Should we have gone straight to Bryant Park or Macy's?

I heard Jillian whisper, "Oh, God, not the Klingon." Her eyes rolled heavenward as she heaved a sigh.

"Zen!" I yelled, interrupting Zen's ranting.

"I can't be*lieve* this," she shouted.

I shrank back from the screen. I felt like my heart was about to jump out of my body when Jillian's warm hand landed on mine and squeezed. Our eyes met and she gave me one more encouraging squeeze. It was just her being a good P.A., right? Or a good friend?

"Sorry, sorry," Zen apologized, rubbing her temples. "You're right that I can track Pole phones, but how did someone get unauthorized access to one? One in every region? Maybe more than one." I could see something between panic and fury flash in her eyes. She looked like she was experiencing her worst nightmare.

"It feels deliberate," I said.

Zen nodded. "I think so, too. I'm going to do some digging, and then I'm going to rope in Rudolph and the Clauses."

I didn't envy her that. This had escalated from a couple of non-believers to a full-on assault on Christmas. I glanced over to see Jillian chewing on her lower lip.

Zen spoke again. "You should go check out Bryant

Park. Just recon—don't get involved. Go observe the Santa and see what kids look like after talking to him. Before you get up tomorrow, we'll have a plan of attack set up for everyone. Good work today, and Jillian, thank your sister. Santa's going to want to add her to the top of the Nice list if she wasn't already there. I'm going to encourage all the reindeer to enlist an elf kid if I can't track the phones. Good work today, both of you."

"Thanks," Jillian said, and I echoed her.

When Zen had hung up, I turned to Jillian. "Do you want to come with me? You don't have to, but—"

Jillian interrupted me. "Yes, but I need to run down to my apartment and grab a few things. Do you mind waiting an hour or so?"

"No, I don't mind. I'll see you in an hour."

Jillian smiled. "It's a date."

At the word *date*, bubbles of happiness floated through my body. Being me, though, of course I started examining my happiness for weaknesses—places where my happiness was too ethereal, and the bubble could pop with the slightest provocation. Like the part where she didn't mean a *date* date. Or the part where she was a friend—my Personal Assistant, in fact. Were reindeer and P.A.s allowed to date? Even so, there was one little bubble of hope that she might like me back, just a little, as more than a friend that I couldn't quite pop.

Chapter Five

*E*ven though I knew it wasn't a real date, I spent the full hour getting ready. I wanted time to try out different outfits. Because reindeers could morph, the apartments had very little in the way of "real" clothes beyond some extra outerwear in the front closet. I stood in front of the mirror I'd discovered on the inside door of the human bedroom closet and morphed through a number of outfits. Red sweater, black jeans? Bor-ring. Blue sweaterdress with silver tights and knee-high boots? Too cute for a mission, and I looked like I was trying too hard. Orange sweater and jeans? I looked like I worked for Halloween, not Christmas. Little black dress? Sexy, and something I'd wear on a real date, but it was a little too exposed for humans in December in New York, and it wasn't a real date. The time passed so swiftly that I'd barely finished deciding on my outfit when I heard the knock at the stall door in the other room.

"Just a second!" I called. I frowned, changed my mind, and morphed my black pants back to jeans. Taking a deep, shaky breath, I went to meet Jillian.

"You look beautiful," said Jillian.

My face burned with pleasure. "Thank you." I'd chosen a fluffy white sweater and jeans with black boots. "So do you."

Jillian looked edible. She was also wearing jeans, but they clung to her curves. The blue plaid flannel shirt matched the sapphire of her eyes. I noticed, for the first time, that her ears were pierced—little gold hoops hung from her lobes. I also noticed a little scar through her eyebrow, and I wondered how that had happened.

The subway was crowded when Jillian and I boarded. There were no seats, so we stood facing each other holding one of the central poles in the car. As the train headed downtown, it filled with more and more humans, pushing Jillian and I closer and closer.

"One more stop." Jillian had leaned into me, so she could speak directly into my ear instead of shouting over the noise. Her breath was warm against my skin. I shivered, wishing I knew if she liked me, even a little. As the train screamed down the track, she gave me a smile. Then she leaned in again. "How do you like the subway?"

Another millimeter and my lips would graze the shell of her ear. "I like flying better."

Her laughter crackled over my skin, making me want.

Our eyes met, and the screeching the train and the chatter of a dozen languages faded away. I felt my tongue wet my suddenly dry lips, and her eyes went molten. She was leaning in, my heart pounding so hard I was shocked it wasn't audible above the cacophony. Then someone pushed past me, shoving me into Jillian's arms. She caught me, our arms instinctively going around each other.

Plastered against Jillian, my heartbeat kicked up to a gallop. Our eyes met, and it was like we were enveloped in one of those snowstorms that make everything hushed and quiet. Her lashes were long, and dark with mascara. She had a light dusting of freckles across her cheeks. Her eyes were a deep blue, almost like a Caribbean Sea. When she licked her lips, my eyes were glued to the action.

I had an irrational thought—I was sure she'd kiss me. The desire was written clearly on her face for anyone to see. I was sure that my own desire was nakedly obvious. She leaned in…

The subway shuddered to a stop. "42nd Street – Bryant Park," crackled the distorted audio.

The moment was over, but I was (mostly) sure I hadn't hallucinated it. Jillian pulled my hand, urging me toward the door before they closed. We stumbled off the subway car, and I blinked owlishly as I tried to reorient myself back to my mission. I was here on a *mission*, and it was *not* to fall for my P.A. But Jillian didn't let go of my hand immediately.

What does that mean?

My romantic experience was pretty limited when it came to elves. I knew how things worked for reindeer. I knew from media the myriad way humans did and didn't work things out in a variety of cultures. But elves? I knew their lives were close-ish to humans, but I didn't know what dating was like for them. I'd had a few reindeer girlfriends, and I'd gone out on a few dates with elves, but not nearly enough to feel like I had a grip on elf dating rituals. Reindeer dates had typically been in reindeer form and usually involved hiking, or occasionally in human forms, trying out human things with another potential. My elven dates had mimicked human dates—dinner or a movie.

If elves just go around holding hands with friends, why didn't they teach us that? I don't have any elf friends I could ask. That's a shame—I wish I could talk to someone about these feelings, and how confused I feel around her.

"Oh, sorry," she said, dropping my suddenly bereft hand.

"It's—" *wonderful, stupendous, magical, and I never want it to stop.* "fine. You're an excellent hand holder," I offered with a smile.

An excellent hand holder? What's wrong with you?

"Any time you have need of my services, I'm available," she said with a flash of those dimples.

I wasn't sure if she meant it or was just flirting. And if it was just flirting, how embarrassing would it be to take her seriously? We'd casually flirted for five seconds while ice skating. Did that mean anything? Deciding it was the safest response, I offered Jillian a small smile.

Bryant Park was breathtaking. A little village of what looked like tiny wooden cottages—some booths, some actual little stores—filled the lawn of the park. Christmas lights twinkled from shop to shop. I saw everything from ornaments to carvings in wood and stone to candles and more. A lovely tree stood in the middle near another public ice-skating rink. The scent of apple cider hung in the air. I stood and observed it for several moments, enjoying the nearly visible Christmas magic of it all.

"Wow."

"I had either this Christmas Village or the one in Union Square bookmarked as activities Wendy would have liked to do for a reason. Sadly, though, it's not why we're here." Jillian sighed.

"You're right. We should find the Santa." I agreed with her.

"We're usually able to get our New York City and Newark elves in as Santa at a lot of New York and New Jersey locations near the city, but this is one of the positions that was filled before our applicant was interviewed. There are at least ten locations we're not in, which is up from only five last year. When hiring season happened, I thought it was a little strange that we didn't get all of our usual Santa placements. Looking back now, it seems pretty fishy. I'm sure I can print out a list of sites without an elf in Manhattan when we get back to the office."

The elves that lived in the human world did a lot of work for Santa. They were recon teams—exploring all the ways in and out of buildings, they monitored construction to let us know where new buildings would be, and around Christmas, the men went out and played Santa. The women had tried, but no one wanted to genderbend Santa, much to everyone's annoyance—including Santa, who would have liked to see a more inclusive approach to Christmas.

"Including Macy's?" I said.

"Yes. We didn't get Macy's this year. One of our elves, Rick, was Santa there for twenty years, but his health has been dicey this year. He's ready to retire to the Pole. But now we need to get our foot in the door all over again," Jillian said. "We can't let Rick find out that the Macy's Santa has been making kids upset—he'll beat himself up over retiring, even though it was the right thing for him to do. I should've thought to share the list of non-elf Santas with you once we heard that a bad Santa was one of the people trying to dissuade believers—it didn't occur to me until just now. I mean, how many other Santas could be doing this?"

"I hear you. Oh, I think I see Santa over there." I pointed.

We strolled over to the little house where "Santa" was meeting children. The Santa looked like a young man in makeup and padding. He was nodding along to a little girl who was speaking animatedly with wide gestures. We made sure to position ourselves near the exit.

In a few moments, the little girl came out and ran over to her mom. "Santa says he's going to put my wish on the list! And he said he bet I was good this year!"

Jillian and I exchanged a look. *Maybe not every kid is getting told*, mine said. *Are we barking up the wrong tree?* hers responded.

"I have an idea," I said. I leaned in and whispered in her ear. "I can turn invisible and go observe. But we need to find a place for me to do that, and I'll need to find somewhere to release the magic to become visible when I'm done."

"Good idea."

Jillian and I looked around and found that the skate rental shop had a small gap behind it that I could fit into. It was poorly lit, which made it a better prospect to avoid detection. I slipped behind the building and used my magic to put up a sight shield.

I followed the children into Santa's hut. Santa reclined in a large golden and red throne, presents arrayed at his feet.

"Next!" the "elf" assistant called to the little boy who looked to be around six at the front of the line.

"Do you want to sit on my lap or next to me?" the Santa asked. Against my will, I approved of the way he didn't force children to sit on his lap.

"Next to you."

The Santa patted the space next to him. "And what's your name?"

"Simon," the little boy said.

"Have you been good this year?" Santa asked.

"Not always," Simon confessed.

Here it was. A perfect opportunity to ruin Christmas magic for a child.

"Aw, I bet you're still on the Nice list," responded the Santa kindly. "What are you hoping for this year?"

Why wasn't he destroying this boy's belief? Could Lee's information from the ice-skating recon have been wrong?

An hour came and went. Child after child—including some high percentage kids—came through, were reassured they were good, and left. Increasingly, I wondered if maybe we were missing something. I returned to the skate rental and dropped the sight shield.

Jillian looked at me expectantly when I returned to her.

"One sec." I waved at her to follow and went around to the front of Santa's hut.

"No cutting the line," one employee said absently, focusing on managing the register.

"Actually, I was wondering if Santa was available to do private parties? How long has he been here?"

A young man in a fleece with a large tree on the front and a nametag that said *Toby* answered my question. "It's his first day. We had issues with our last Santa." He glanced both ways, then leaned in and whispered, "He made some kids cry. I mean, what's up with that?"

"Oh, man," I replied.

This dude is like a ghost. Where would we look for him now?

"Right?" he responded. "Anyway, this new guy seems great. If you wait until six-thirty, his shift is over and you can ask him about parties."

"That's great, thanks," I said with genuine sincerity. Kids deserved a good Santa, even as I desperately wanted to catch the person out to ruin Christmas.

Jillian looked dejected. "Terrible luck."

"We should talk to Zen," I said.

"Do you want me to get the list of non-elf Santas? We could maybe start going through it—" she glanced at her phone. "It's a bit late, six p.m. already. We probably can't make any of the other Santas around the city—they usually stop between six and seven, and we'd have to take the subway during rush hour. Maybe ask Zen if she wants us to go to all those sites tomorrow? Here, I'll forward you my spreadsheet and you can send that on to Zen." She pulled out her phone and sent the email in moments. I was someone who appreciated organization, but Jillian was organized on a whole other level.

I nodded. We found a quiet, out-of-the-way corner of the park. I pulled my phone out to email Zen, attaching the spreadsheet, while Jillian stepped away to get us something to drink. Once I finished my email, I put the phone back in human mode.

"Here you go," Jillian said, offering me the cider.

It was deliciously hot as it made its way down my throat. Sweet, hot, and a little spicy. Perfect.

"Thanks," I said.

Jillian winked at me and gestured. "Hey, look, it's a you."

I glanced at the booth and laughed. The little cottage was full to the brim with ornaments, but reindeer themed ones were front and center. Some were of Rudolph, complete with red nose. I had heard a rumor—although I had no idea how true it was—that Rudolph hated the song and being pictured with the nose. I knew she flew with a high-powered light on her chest, not her nose. But the rest of the reindeer ornaments had black noses—one of which I *had* to buy.

"Excuse me. I know we're on our mission, but I need one of those," I said to Jillian and stepped up to buy it.

"No worries! You should have a little fun. We can't do much more with the mission tonight."

A few moments later, I was back.

"So what's the mysterious ornament you needed?" Jillian said with a smile.

"Zen loves Star Trek, so this reindeer in a red shirt is perfect for her. I've only seen a little Star Trek, but I recognize this from the show and some memes. I don't know many of the reindeer, but she tried to make me feel included." *She gave me a nickname. She wants me to feel like part of the team.*

Jillian smiled. "I like that. I know Zen can rub people the wrong way, so it's great that you guys are getting along. So…let me guess. I don't think you're the gymnast reindeer, although you could be cartwheeling through the apartment at night. I don't know any reindeer who play soccer. I bet you're the skiing reindeer."

"Nope. None of the above."

"Which one are you, then?"

Without thinking, I said, "The one who has panic attacks." Then I covered my mouth, horror flooding my body. "Please don't tell anyone about that. What if they take me off the team? I don't think people with panic attacks get to be on the team."

"Claudia, you may have panic attacks, but you are on top of everything this year. I believe your anxiety is real, and it's something you deal with, but it's not all you are. Tell me an obsession you have with media, like how Zen likes Star Trek."

"I like musicals," I said. "My shower is quite the Broadway stage. I get a standing ovation every day."

She burst into peals of laughter. "You like musicals and you haven't asked me about seeing a Broadway show?"

"Well, you had everything planned, and then this whole believer thing happened. I thought maybe I'd come back to New York after the Big Show." I glanced at her, then looked away. "I mean, if it's okay with you. I'll be out of the apartment for the most part. I want to go see *Six* and *Wicked*, and to go to TKTS and pick a show on the fly. But I never thought I'd do that now—I only have a week. Not even a week now."

She used her free hand to brush some of my hair behind my ear. "I would *love* if you came back."

"I wouldn't bother you," I promised.

"Claudia, you are anything but a bother," she said.

"Oh, there's an answer from Zen. She says, 'We'll find out more in the morning. You should go out dancing or just take a break tonight.'"

"Do you want to enjoy the Christmas village here? Or we could go look at more department store windows—those were high on Wendy's list. Or we could—"

"I'd like to stay here," I said. "But I'm really touched that you are trying to think of a way to make my time here special."

At first it seemed as if Jillian were struggling for words. "Well, I— You should know that I— I hope you have a magical first year here." She looked a little bereft. I wanted to say or do something, but I couldn't figure out what, so I stayed silent.

We wandered up and down the aisles. There was a stall selling carved candles where I picked one up for my mother. She loved unique candles, and this green one carved to look like a Christmas Tree was perfect. Atop it sat a golden star. Someone had gone back with colored wax and added "lights." I just knew she'd love receiving this. And that it was from my first big mission would make it all the more special to her.

"You know," I said as we wandered up and down the aisle. "It's so strange that each of us is having a problem in the city we have our headquarters—well except Zen. And even that seems intentional."

"Because she's the tech whiz?" Jillian asked.

"Yeah. How better to divide her focus on the N-o-N breach than to have her attention bouncing between Singapore and Hong Kong?"

Jillian chewed her lower lip. "That *is* suspicious. And you're right, she's the only one."

The subject lapsed, but I continued to chew over it in the back of my mind.

I stopped at a stall with cloud-soft knitted baby blankets. Looking over the blankets—and maybe petting them a little—I selected one turquoise and one purple. That and the ornament were nice thank-you-for-your-kindness gifts for Wendy. Poor substitutes for her missing out on her time in New York. Selfishly, I was glad because otherwise I'd never have met Jillian.

"Who are those for?" Jillian looked surprised by my purchases.

"Wendy. The real Comet, I mean. She's been nothing but kind and supportive. She could be focusing on her pregnancy, but she's still acting as part of the team and she's just as invested in solving this mystery as we are. But despite all of that, she's made herself available to me." I said. I kind of wanted to be Wendy when I grew up—a calm, steady, and *confident* team member.

"You're the real Comet, too, you know. But we should send something to her from the elves, too," Jillian mused.

"I bet she'd like that." We walked in companionable silence toward the subway for a little while, then I turned to her. "Jillian, can I ask you about growing up here?"

"Of course. I'm an open book for you, Claudia," she said.

"It's just, you're nothing like the people at the Pole. But not in a bad way!"

"We aren't. I struggled when I was at the Pole, and I

was pretty relieved to get back here," she said. "If I get the job with Rudolph, that will be the hardest part. I know I can spend my off months here, but being away from my family—especially Lee—and my home culture will be really lonely. You and the team members will be the only people I know there. Maybe you can be my guide and show me all the ways of the Pole."

See, just friends. That's all there is here.

"I think the Pole will take some getting used to, but I'm sure you'd grow to find it feels like home. I'd be happy to help!" Did I sound too eager?

We'll have to skip the bridge to the ice-skating rink. It has mistletoe hanging all along it. You're supposed to give a quick kiss to your friend as you cross, but I don't want a friendly kiss from Jillian. I want the real thing.

Jillian didn't seem to notice my distraction. "It would definitely be a huge adjustment. But if you can adjust to being a team member without notice, I can adjust to living at the Pole six or so months a year."

"Did you play with human kids the way Lee does? Playdates and all that?" I asked.

"Yes. I still have human friends. They think I'm the executive assistant to a big deal CEO."

"I'm a big deal CEO? Quite the promotion," I said.

She snorted. "I don't know. Your current job title is pretty impressive."

"I dreamed of it my whole life. I can't believe it's real," I confessed.

Despite everything—my anxiety, my crush on Jillian, new non-believers—this was the highlight of my twenty-five years. I was living out my dreams. Flying and seeing cities from the sky, circling the Statue of Liberty, prancing down through the sky to land on the roof were all things I could only have dreamt about last week.

Underneath my fear that I wasn't the right reindeer for the job and that Wendy or someone else would be handling all of this better was a growing sense of rightness. Maybe I wasn't a complete fraud. It was only a spark right now, but I wondered if it might eventually grow into the blaze that Wendy and the others all seemed to nurture—I bet Wendy never thought she was a fake.

"You're doing a great job," Jillian said.

"Thanks. I guess you think of home as being New York City rather than the Pole?"

"Hmmm. Yes, in a very real way, because it's familiar. It's where I've spent twenty-seven of the last twenty-eight years of my life. But honestly, each has its pros and cons. This is home, but I have to hide who I really am. The Pole is great too, in that I don't ever have to hide who I really am, and I get to really embrace that. And I like ice skating year round, and getting to know other elves and snowmen and all that. It's just…it feels alien—and I don't feel like I fit in. But you're right that that would change with some time. And you'll show me around your home, right? And if you do decide to come back to New York, I'd love to show you around my home."

"That would be amazing!"

Back at the apartment, Jillian walked me to the stall. I put away the bag with the gifts in the human bedroom closet. When I did, I saw the shirt I'd bought for Jillian. I took a deep breath to calm my nerves.

"Jillian, can you wait a second?" I called out.

"Sure." She sounded surprised.

Shyly, I crossed to her. "I wanted to give you this," I said, holding up the t-shirt.

"You didn't have to," she said as she accepted the gift with a dimpled smile. Damn those dimples for being so irresistible! They made my stomach flutter and my heart shiver. "I don't have anything in return."

"You know that gifts aren't meant to be an obligation," I gently chided her. It was one of the maxims of the Pole.

"You're right," she agreed.

"Besides, you're doing so much more than your job. I don't know why you're doing so much more for me than you have to," I said. "You could be like the reindeer who just want to keep things professional. I don't know why you're so kind to me, but I'm grateful."

She let out a deep sigh. "I'd like to think I'd be kind to anyone, but, Claudia, do you really not know why I'm like this around you?"

I felt like I was failing a test. I hadn't done the reading. What was I missing?

"I—? I don't know?" I stammered.

She gently brushed her hand over my cheek. "I've been trying to drop hints. Look, I know I'm overstepping all kind of boundaries, but I like you. If you're not interested, I'll never—"

But she never finished the sentence. Because I'd thrown caution to the wind and put a finger over her lips. She stopped, and watched me.

"I'm interested, Jillian. I really like you." I moved my finger and stepped closer.

Her arms came around me, one curved about my waist, the other a comforting pressure rubbing up and down my back. It was like she could sense how inexperienced I was with elves. I twined my arms around her neck. When our eyes locked, I could swear Jillian's eyes got bluer the longer I looked. My world shrank to the two of us.

The first brushes of her lips were hesitant. A question to be answered that sent a shiver over my skin. I answered with my own chaste kisses. She let the kiss turn a little warmer, sweet open-mouthed kisses that sent delight up and down my spine.

Jillian's tongue touched my lips and I opened for her. Her hand slid up to hold the nape of my neck. I answered with all of my eagerness, inviting her into my mouth, our tongues caressing and sliding against each other. Teeth nipped my lower lip and I couldn't hold back a moan, which Jillian echoed. I clung to Jillian and kissed her back eagerly over and over.

Some kisses are a snow flurry—a fun little burst of snow beneath a sunny sky. Other kisses are a heavy snow—solid and comforting. Then there are blizzards—all consuming, inspiring the desire to snuggle down with a loved one to exclusion of all else. Until tonight I would've said that I'd had blizzard kisses. I had only just realized those weren't blizzards—this was. I had lost all sense of up and down, which should be impossible for a being who always knows exactly where she is in space at any given moment.

When we separated, I felt a little woozy. Jillian looked similarly unsteady on her feet.

"That was— Claudia, was it— For you too?" Jillian managed.

"It was everything," I answered, my breathing still unsteady.

"I want to get to know you better. And I want to kiss you again," Jillian said, her breathing still not quite back to normal.

"I feel the same way. I want to know all about you. And I definitely want to kiss you some more." I could feel the smile stretching across my face. *She liked me!*

Jillian reached for one of my hands, and I held it while little sparks of electricity crackled over my skin. The other slid behind my neck, caressing sensitized skin. I wrapped my free arm around her waist and tilted my head. When her mouth settled over mine, hot and demanding, I yanked her tighter against me until we were plastered against each other the way we'd been on the subway; this time intentionally and passionately.

My back met the wall of the stall as Jillian pressed me against it. My hand fisted in her shirt, and she gave a little growl of encouragement. When her lips traveled up so she could nibble at my ear, a delicious scent tickled my nose. Where the last time she had smelled lightly of citrus, this time she smelled earthy. I buried my face in her shoulder and couldn't hold back a squeak of desire.

We froze when a phone pinged.

"It could be about the mission." My whisper was as loud as a shout in the quiet.

Jillian swore lightly under her breath, and I wholeheartedly agreed with the sentiment.

"Right," she finally said after several long breaths.

We separated and glanced at our phones.

Jillian winced. "I do actually need to answer this email. I would love nothing more than to stay here with you and keep kissing you…" her voice trailed off.

I nodded. "I agree. I'd like nothing more than to keep kissing you, too. But I get it. You need to be responsible." I looked at my phone again. "And yikes. It's getting late."

"Goodnight, Claudia," Jillian said with a kiss that almost lasted a little too long. Another ten seconds and we would have been against the wall again.

"Night, Jillian," I said with a kiss to her cheek. I didn't trust myself to kiss her lips again.

I morphed and settled down, confident that tonight would be free of stress dreams.

Chapter Six

Following my nose, I found Jillian in the kitchen, watching the coffee maker as if it were about to share the secrets of the universe. I was a little selfishly glad that everyone else was at the Pole with Rudolph, planning the worldwide route.

"Good morning," I said shyly.

Jillian looked up and gave me a wide smile. Her voice was flirty in a way that made me glow inside. "Hi, you. Can I kiss you?"

"I'd like that."

She cradled my face as gently as you would a spun-glass ornament. Her kiss was sweet, and all too brief. "Have you heard from Blitzen?"

I glanced at the phone. "No, not yet."

She handed me the first cup of coffee. "Lee is hoping we need her again. Working with us yesterday made her feel so special."

I smiled. "I can relate. I've spent my whole life wanting to help the Pole. And now they're letting me help guide the sleigh this year and next."

"Then what?"

"I don't know what will happen. I'm trying to enjoy every minute I have."

"Why for only two years?"

"The real Comet—Wendy—is having babies. Well, you knew that. She's too pregnant to fly this year, and next year the babies will be too little. But the year after that? If she wants to be Comet again, it's her job to have. I'm hoping for something that will give me time on the team after next year. Maybe a retirement."

Jillian bit her lip. "Too bad they couldn't just add you to the team."

"*Ten* reindeer? That would be sacrilege. It's eight reindeer plus Rudolph. The song says so," I teased. "All joking aside, guiding the sleigh, even if only twice, is the honor of my lifetime."

"I'm truly happy for you. Do you want breakfast?"

"Yes. I'm starving!"

"What would you like to try that you've never had before? I'm not the best chef, but I can make a lot of different breakfast foods," Jillian offered.

"Pancakes?" I'd had some of the typical elf food on dates and as part of the training program, but that was different. There wasn't a huge amount of variety in the typical elf diet at the Pole. I was more curious about all this unfamiliar human food.

I should really tell them it's a weakness of the training program. We don't get to try human food, really. And elf food and human food are different—human food is so varied.

Pole food was more like a Nordic diet than an American one. I'd had rugbrod, the dense sourdough rye bread, lots of fatty fish, and more root vegetables than I necessarily ever wanted again. Any sweets associated with Santa were also eaten, so lots of peppermint and gingerbread, but not so much when it came to steak or rice. Call me ungrateful but I wanted to try pizza, bulgogi, and rogan josh instead. I guess we always look down on the familiar.

"I can make pancakes. Plain, chocolate chip, or blueberry?"

"Chocolate chip sounds great."

"Want to help?" Jillian asked.

Jillian and I worked together in the gleaming kitchen. I put on an apron that said *Life is too short; Lick the bowl.* Jillian talked me through measuring the ingredients and was patient as I worked slowly to measure as accurately as possible.

There was a crack as Jillian broke an egg one-handed.

"Show-off," I teased. "I wish I could do that."

She winked at me.

As I stirred the batter, Jillian heated a skillet. At her direction, I dropped batter on the pan, and added some chocolate chips.

"I want to show off for real," she said as we watched the pancake cook. "Can I?"

"Sure," I handed her the turner.

She took the turner and placed it on the counter. With a cocky grin, she lifted the pan and jiggled it in small back-and-forth movements, loosening the pancake from the surface of the pan. She gave the pan an upward jerk and the pancake flew into the air, flipped, and landed batter side down to finish cooking.

"Okay, I'm impressed."

"Let's hope you still think that when you eat them," she said with a confident air. She already knew I'd love them.

We ate our pancakes at the table in the quiet dining room off of the living room. She talked more about growing up in New York. At nine she'd gone to see *The Lion King*, and I couldn't help but be jealous. She'd seen a number of shows I wanted to see in person, so we spent the rest of breakfast talking about theater.

After breakfast, there still wasn't an email. Jillian and I parted ways to each work independently.

I was glad for the opportunity. Something Jillian had said last night was playing on repeat in my head—that telling me she liked me was overstepping boundaries. Were any of the boundaries ones we'd get in trouble for crossing? I'd been worried that flirting with her was inappropriate. How bad was kissing? Dating? I couldn't remember anything about interoffice romance from my briefings. I'd foolishly assumed it would never apply to me and let the knowledge fade from my mind as irrelevant. Not so smart of me.

I decided to take a risk.

"Claudia! How are you, honey?" Wendy's smile was wide and welcoming.

"I'm good. I'm waiting for an email from Zen to tell us what the Pole wants us to do next."

"I don't envy you all the intrigue."

"I, um, wanted to ask you something. But it has to be just between us. Do you promise?" I felt my confidence in this plan waver.

She frowned. "Of course. Is everything okay?"

"Um, is it allowed for a reindeer and an elf to…date?" I asked, feeling my face burn as I asked it.

She laughed. "So, the fair Jillian has caught your eye?"

"I— I—" I took a deep breath. "Yes. Jillian."

"Keep things private until after the Big Show, but who's there to see it? After the Big Show it's not like she'd be your PA again for years. It's a little naughty to hook up before the Big Show, but I'd be lying if I didn't say it hasn't happened before. All of us are in our—Sorry, all of you are in your regions with just the P.A.s and the elves that do unrelated jobs, like playing Santa. Everyone else is at the Pole—Rudolph has commissioned one of the elf training rooms that can hold several hundred people and is using Zen's 3D imaging to plan the trip while everyone weighs in on what the best routes are. I hear it's quite lively over there."

I nodded. We talked several more minutes, but then I got an alert that Blitzen had sent me a new email, so we hung up. Zen had added another feature to my phone to track the type of Pole phone that Jillian and I had, with N-o-N capabilities. I could see two in New York that didn't belong to either me or Jillian. Our mission was to track down one of the two Pole phones and to try to get it back.

One of the phones was at Macy's. That definitely seemed like the Santa we'd been warned about. The other was nearby, just across the park at the Metropolitan Museum of Art.

"Jillian, why don't we go after this one first? They're close by and won't be surrounded by people the way the Santa at Macy's will be. The only way we can go after the Santa is if Lee came, and I am not comfortable putting her in contact with someone who is talented at making people lose their belief."

"It's a good plan. Let's go recover a phone!"

The Met was a massive museum full of works of art, many obtained without permission. I was so conflicted because on one hand, *omg, mummies!* On the other was the fact that Egypt hadn't been consulted when the mummies were taken out of Egypt. Our phone thief was loitering by the statue *Hatshepsut seated* in the Egyptian wing.

He looked to be about our age, somewhere in his mid-to-late twenties. I judged him to be about a head taller than me. He had thick curly brown hair sticking out from under a Yankees cap, and shockingly green eyes.

"Now what?" Jillian murmured as we surreptitiously watched him.

I'd been inspired to bring my "petition" with us. After all, it had worked once before, hadn't it? I pulled it out of a backpack I'd found in the front closet. "Now I go talk to him."

Breathe in for four, Breathe out for four. Relax my shoulders. Yawn to loosen the jaw.

All tricks to manage the way my body tightened up when I was anxious. Prepared, I walked across the gallery to him

"Excuse me, sir?" I asked.

"Oh, hi," he said in return.

"My name is Charlotte. I'm with New Yorkers Across the Holidays." I lied smoothly. This was something I *did* have to practice at school—how to lie convincingly. Every reindeer needed to know how to do it or we'd have exposed Christmas magic long ago. I started to give him my spiel about what "we" were hoping our petition would create.

"Hey, Charlotte. I'm Travis." He interrupted me. "That's an interesting cause. Tell you what—you tell me more about your cause, and then we hang out for a little while?" He raised an eyebrow in invitation.

Is he hitting on me? It feels weird.

"Sure." I agreed with a convincingly fake smile.

"So when did you get involved?"

"Oh, just this year. But I love the idea of helping kids have a happy holiday. We're proposing a craft fair where kids make crafts and sell them, and then they use the money to pay for holiday events."

"Do you do a lot of activism for kids?" he asked.

"Sort of. I work for a company that focuses on kids."

"So this fair—what about schools that don't have enough technology?"

"I— It's sad."

He nodded. "I just think that ensuring schools are well supplied is so much more important. Don't you agree?"

Maybe he has a point?

What? No! No, he doesn't have a point! Or, well, much of one, I conceded.

"Joy is also important. They can have fun with the money they raise from the fair."

He shook his head. "Fun believing in Santa?"

"Of course! Don't you believe in Santa?" I protested.

He scoffed. "I'm not a child. Are you seriously telling me that at twenty-what? Twenty-three? Twenty-four? That you still believe?"

There was a lot I loved about the human world. The way non-believers acted as though believing was stupid or childish was something I found disheartening.

"I think you're never too old to believe," I said.

He took a phone out of his pocket. "Hey, can I take your picture? The cute girl who tried to get me to believe?"

I could tell it was the Pole phone because of the way it was slightly blurry, the same way the rooftop door appeared to my eyes. This was a phone that could use Christmas magic. Why would he take my picture?

To look me up on the list!

"I—"

"C'mon, Charlotte, it's Christmas. Spread some holiday cheer and smile for the camera."

"Okay," I agreed weakly. My pancakes rose up as he took my picture and started clicking through his phone.

"Oh yeah, this is one for the Gram," he said with a wink. A few second later, he frowned. "Weird."

"What's weird?"

"Nothing." He said it too quickly. I couldn't remember the N-o-N specifying species, but I'd never thought about it. I wondered if I was a tabula rasa to the N-o-N, since it tracked humans. I hoped that I was. Otherwise he was reading that I was a reindeer, which was a significantly worse outcome.

I pulled out my Pole phone. "Turn about is fair play." I snapped a photo and got his data immediately.

Travis Feehan, age twenty-six, nine years on the good list, one year on the naughty list, non-believer since the age of ten.

"Come look at the temple with me." he said. It wasn't a question, and my hackles rose although I gave a smile that made me nauseous and made him smile like he knew that I'd be free only if he deigned to ask me out.

Sorry I mouthed over my shoulder at Jillian.

She shook her head and mouthed *don't worry, it's okay* at me.

On the walk to the temple Travis told me he was from Oklahoma. He'd come to school here—NYU. He was working on a Ph.D. in English Literature in the 19th century. He made sure to tell me several times that he was single, which made me want to roll my eyes and say "well, duh!" but I didn't. I said I was single, too, which was technically true—and the only true thing I said, but I hoped that maybe I wouldn't be for much longer.

We sat near the water and looked at the temple.

"So, big believer in the Nice list?" he asked.

"Yes."

"Doesn't it bug you to buy presents for people? Having to find the perfect the gift?" Travis said.

"No, I like thinking about people and finding the right gift."

"You're one of those people who finish shopping before

Thanksgiving, aren't you?" He made the accusation in a joking tone of voice.

"I am."

I usually was done with Christmas gifts by Halloween. If you placed your orders in a timely fashion, you never had to pick from what was left over after the elves finished apportioning out gifts to the believers and those at the Pole who had gotten their orders in first.

"Have a heart for us last-minute shoppers, beautiful. Do you know how stressful it is to buy for everyone at the last minute? Don't you hate how crowded and claustrophobic stores get? Even Amazon slows down its deliveries, so sometimes I have no choice but to do it in person."

"What about the look of pleasure on someone's face?"

"What about how it feels when that is a look of disappointment?"

"I imagine that's rough," I said sympathetically. "It's really unkind, though. I was taught that gifts aren't obligations. They are something to be grateful for, even if it might not be something you'd pick out on your own."

"Yeah, that's not how my family operates. Sorry, babe. It's getting late, I should go." Travis looked at his phone and grimaced.

"I'll walk you to the exit." I offered.

I can't let that phone go!

My heart was pounding in my ears as I followed Travis, casually flirting all the while. He made me uncomfortable, but the only thing I was invested in was him buying my lies. We made our way down the stairs from the museum to the street. Once we were standing on 5th avenue, I glanced up around and saw Jillian on the stairs. She spread her arms as if to say *I have no idea what you should do next.*

"Here, give me your phone. I'll put in my number and call myself so I have your number and you have mine." It was a desperate gamble. I had no plan. I just knew I needed to get my hands on his phone.

Travis handed it over to me. The light changed and people streamed across the street. Slowly, I entered in a fake number, my hand squeezing the phone in a death grip. The crosswalk started making a keening noise to alert pedestrians that the countdown to a light change was down to five. I turned and ran, bounding across the lanes of traffic just as the light changed and the traffic surged forward.

"Hey! She stole my phone! Hey, stop!"

My feet pounded on the pavement, running as fast as I dared. Tourists and locals were merely obstacles to dodge as I turned left. I charged down the street, sure he'd be after me as soon as he could.

I cut between two buildings into an alley. The first order of business was to get a sight shield up. I looked around and, seeing the coast was clear, put one up. Hidden from view, I took both phones and put them into the backpack with the petition. Then I morphed, picked up the backpack with my teeth, and took off into the sky.

When I landed at headquarters, I kept my sight shield up until inside. Once I was in the familiar setting, I dropped it and sagged against the wall. The adrenaline leeched out of my body, leaving me exhausted. I went to the living room of the apartment and dropped on the couch to text Jillian where I was.

I video-called Zen to tell her I had one of the phones. I assumed I would just leave a message, but she picked up, even though it was around five a.m. in her region.

"Good. Bring it to me, please? Use the transporter. Have Jillian send you to Singapore."

"What about the other phone?"

"I want to see the one you have first. You're the only

person who has gotten their hands on one. How did you manage it?"

I felt my face burn. "Um, I was pretending to give him my number and then I just stole it and ran away."

Zen burst out laughing. "Oh, Kid Comet, that is going to be one of my favorite stories for years to come."

If even possible, my face heated further, and I ducked my head a little in embarrassment.

Zen's whole demeanor changed. "Hey, no! Don't feel bad. I'm really proud of you, and I wish I could pull that off."

Jillian walked into the apartment, and when she saw me, she gave me a little wave. "I'll have Jillian send me to you. When should I come?"

"Now is good."

I explained to Jillian where I needed to go and why. We went to the transporter room—each headquarters and a few other buildings in each region had a dedicated transporter. This one was in a labeled room. The walls were painted a muted silver. A large silver podium dominated the room and clashed with the golden floors. Near one of the windows was a touch-screen display to control the transporter. I wondered how much of the setup was necessary and what Zen might have added for her own amusement. It did look a lot like the few episodes of Star Trek I'd seen.

The sensation of being transported was like having your stomach jump up into your chest while every inch of your skin itched.

The first impression I had of Singapore was the slap of heat and humidity that told me I was no longer in New York.

The second impression I had was that my body was on

fire with an uncontrollable itch. I immediately started scratching with my free hand.

Zen was there to meet me. "Sorry! I forgot to warn you! The sensation only lasts about five minutes, but it's an itchy five minutes. Here, give me your phone and the fake phone. Then chill out and don't scratch. Try local snacks—sorry, it's early so we don't have much food ready. Do you like toast?" When I nodded, she looked to an elf. "Can you make Comet some Kaya toast, Wei Liang?"

"Sure. This way," Wei Liang said, leading me to a living room with floor to ceiling windows. I was distracted from the itching, although one hand still rubbed the opposite arm—I very nearly almost pressed my nose to the window. It was a busy urban street, but there was green everywhere and flowers rioted from an overhead walkway that allowed pedestrians to safely cross the many lanes of traffic. Buildings with orange tiled roofs were in one direction, gleaming skyscrapers in the other. Despite the early hour, it was already hot enough that I morphed my winter wear away in favor of a light maxi sundress and bare feet like Zen, and Wei Liang.

A few minutes later, Wei Liang offered me an already sweating bottle of cold water, and what looked like a little toast sandwich "Claudia, right?"

I was shocked to hear him address me as Claudia.

"Yes. How did you know?" I asked.

"Wendy told me—she's one of my best friends. How's it going?" he asked as he sat down next to me.

"I think it's going as well as possible. I can see why Wendy is sad to miss New York City at Christmas."

"People will trade regions if she still wants that experience when she comes back." He didn't seem concerned.

I felt a little pang at the reminder that I was a temporary fixture on the team. I knew that when Wendy wanted to come back, I would have to step away. As it should be. The job was Wendy's, not mine. But what would that mean for me? Would I go back to not leaving the Pole? Could I join the team that monitors humans, and do some flying that way? They'd never used reindeer, but maybe they could?

And what about Jillian? Was there a future there?

Not today's problem.

"Ghuy'cha'!" A shout in what had to be Klingon echoed down the hall from where Zen was working. I didn't need to know that language, though, to understand when someone was swearing.

"Is she okay?" I looked at Wei Liang with concern.

"That's just Zen." Wei Liang shrugged it off.

I took a bite of the food and was immediately distracted. "Wow, this is good!" The jam in the toast sandwiches was rich tasting, with a deep saltiness that was offset by sweetness.

"Kaya toast—butter and a kaya jam made of eggs and coconut. A lot of locals drink it with tea or coffee, but I thought you might prefer water after your first transport. Some people feel a little queasy. But you know—you should try chili crab your next time you're here. Local delicacy, and if you can handle spice, it's perfect. Wendy said you'd really liked trying pizza," Wei Liang said.

"I think I could happily spend all my free time eating. Except I also want to go to see shows and museums and sports and everything. I want to do it all at once."

He laughed. "Wendy was like that at first, too."

"We're all like that at first. Then we remember we have all the time in the world, and learn to pace ourselves," Zen said from the doorway. "I know what happened. This isn't a Pole phone."

"But it's blurry—" I began.

Zen cut me off. "It's a clone of a Pole phone. Whoever is behind this has at least one real Pole phone, and then used magic to clone it. I've gone through my records. In the last five years, twenty-four phones have been lost by elves. But only four phones have been lost by reindeer or P.A.'s in the real world with the N-o-N installed on it. I was never able to find three of them when I went to brick them. But in two of the three cases, the person was near water, so I had to assume the phones went in the water. I sent elves back to check and no one found anything. I had convinced myself and Rudolph *and* the Clauses that the final phone had been run over by a car or something. How could I be such a stupid *petaQ?*"

I watched her pace, her hands running through hair that was starting to stand up wildly on its own after too many times.

"Zen, maybe—"

She turned toward me, her eyes a little wild. "What?"

"Let me get the other phone. Maybe we can catch the person and find out where they got theirs? If the mastermind can clone phones endlessly, then they'll just keep doing that, right? But if we know who it is…"

Zen nodded. "Okay Comet, here's how it's going to go down. You and Jillian are kicking ass and taking names, but I don't want you to risk running from cops again. If you go to Macy's, you can take his picture and get his name. Once we have his name, we can get an address. I don't want a public confrontation with a Santa, even a bad, fake Santa."

I was transported back to New York. Jillian had left the apartment, but I remembered her invitation to hang out from earlier and texted her once the hellish itching receded. The Santaland at Macy's had closed for the day, so that would have to wait until tomorrow morning.

"Since we're finding ourselves with a quiet night, I'd like to end today with a date. Your choice—go out and explore or stay in and watch Netflix." Jillian said after returning to the penthouse. She bit her lip as she waited for my response.

"Staying in sounds amazing." I leaned forward and brushed a kiss on her cheek. After all the intrigue of the day, I didn't want crowds.

We put on *Queer Eye*, which I hadn't seen, although I'd heard of it. I asked Jillian to order her favorite food, and by the end of the first episode we had New York style Chinese food. The teriyaki beef skewers were my favorite —the almost sweet flavor had me reaching for more, but I also liked the crispiness that gave way to the softness of the scallion pancakes and the contrast of the vegetables and the grains of the fried rice.

While trading childhood stories I learned that her scar through her eyebrow was from an accident while sock skating.

"Sock skating?" I asked.

"When you run and then try to slide in your socks over a hardwood or marble floor. I was sliding and hit a doorframe. Very bloody. Very dramatic," Jillian rolled her eyes at the memory. "What about you?"

"I had my own bit of drama." I indicated my right arm where there were several scars, one of them quite long. "I broke this pretty badly. I tried to climb a tree, and I fell out of it. I had to have two surgeries, and there's a pin in there. That was pretty scary. And on top of everything, I couldn't morph for nearly three months, which meant I fell behind a bit in my classes."

"You must have hated that. But clearly you caught up —you're the top potential team member if you got tapped."

"It wasn't a highlight of my youth. This, however," I said gesturing at the space between us, "is the best part of being in New York."

Jillian laced her fingers between mine. "I think so, too." She reached behind herself with her other hand and pulled out a large red fleece blanket. "Want to cuddle?"

"I'd really like that."

Her dimples appeared at my words.

Happily, I scooted over until we were a hair's breadth apart. She moved the blanket so it was draped over both our laps. Looking up into her blue eyes, I thought about last night. How much I'd like a repeat.

I brushed a stray lock of hair behind her ear. The blonde strands were just as silky as I'd expected. I saw her swallow, her eyes growing hot with desire. She leaned toward me, her eyebrow arching, asking me what was okay, and my lips met hers eagerly.

When her mouth brushed mine, I sank into the warm confection of my desire. It was sweet and deep like an endless vat of caramel. I could hear the ticking clock, then, as her kisses overwhelmed me, the sound melted away until the only sounds were our breath, growing heavy with anticipation of what came next. I gave her hungry kisses, my tongue entreating hers to play.

We'd had a fast peck when Jillian had arrived, but nothing since, and I was a starving woman. The intensity of my desire was surprising—it was like I'd fallen under a spell. So much was changing, including me, but Jillian was like this warm and comforting presence. She was beautiful, kind, and smart. But she wasn't just warm, she was red hot —every time I looked at her, there was a flutter low in my belly.

A week ago, I would have wondered what she saw in me, but I was starting to get an inkling of what it could be.

I wasn't the same reindeer I'd been a week ago, when being a team member was a far-off dream.

Our fingers entwined, squeezed, then released so we could reach for each other. She slid a hand into my hair to angle my head the way she wanted it. Then her teeth scraped the side of my neck and I moaned. Jillian gathered me close, and her lips possessed mine again—who needed oxygen when I had Jillian?

Had yesterday's kiss been a blizzard? This was a bomb cyclone. If I wasn't careful, I'd fall for Jillian, and fast. I was halfway in love with her already.

My stall felt lonely that night. I ended up morphing on pajamas and trying out the bed. It was just as soft as it looked. But it was equally lonely.

Chapter Seven

*I*t was time to go to Macy's.

I wasn't prepared. I objectively knew how big the store was, and that it would be crowded. But I wasn't prepared.

I flinched for roughly the tenth time since we'd entered the store when I got shoved, again, by someone's collection of bags as they tried to maneuver through the crowd. Christmas music blasted aggressively—Zen would have been losing her mind. There were people everywhere, and between the music, and the voices, and the beeps and chirps of cash registers it was a wall of sound. Jillian looked at me and offered her hand, which I grabbed like the lifeline it was.

Finally, we got to "Santaland," a holiday wonderland on the eighth floor of Macy's. Everywhere I looked I saw something. Over here, the "Domino Sugar Bake Shop" was decorated like a gingerbread house. Over there a pig in a tutu twirled next to a tree. I loved the extensive toy trains running on complicated looking tracks. There were even animatronic polar bears!

"This is incredible!" I exclaimed, thoroughly charmed.

"If you like this, you'll love Bloomingdale's. I know this is the stereotypical ultimate Santa experience, but I like Bloomingdale's better," Jillian said.

We followed a whimsical path over a "rainbow bridge." The buildings we were passing were supposed to be part of the elves' workshop—windows overlooked animatronic scenes where elves got presents ready for Santa. Just before the Santa meet-and-greet, there was one last big decoration—a golden sleigh with which children could pose for photos. The real sleigh was red with golden runners, and it was about four or five times as big as this model.

Finally, though, we found the big fake himself, the bad Santa Claus.

He was perched on a wooden bench with a green cushion. Reindeer flanked a painted Christmas tree on the back of his throne. Although the make-up was much better, I could see that this Santa was also young, although possibly not as young as the Santa we'd found at Bryant Park.

I noticed a little boy waiting in line without a grown-up. He looked to be all of six or seven. I glanced at my phone, flicking it into Pole mode—Josh Allen, age seven, consistently on the Nice list, second year at the top of the list. His eyes were wide as he took in the spectacle of Santaland.

"Let's hang out over there for a while," I said, taking Jillian by the hand and pulling her near the exit of the Santa meet-up.

The first few kids were fine. They demonstrated the kind of excitement and happiness that a child *should* have when they meet Santa. Then Josh came out of the meet-up, eyes brimming with tears. I looked for his grown-up, but he was still alone.

"Josh?"

"Claudia, stop! What are you doing?" Jillian hissed.

What I have to do. What's right.

"Who are you?" He didn't seem scared of me, but he did seem confused that I was talking to him.

"I'm one of Santa's helpers. Why are you sad?"

"There's no Santa. *He* told me so," Josh said, swatting away a tear that had spilled onto his cheek.

"Who cares what he says? He's not the real Santa," I said recklessly. I would not let Josh stop believing. Not if I could stop it. "You want a stuffed lioness for Christmas, don't you?"

His mouth fell open. "How did you know that? I even told that Santa that I wanted a Nintendo Switch."

"I told you I'm one of Santa's—the real Santa's—helpers. You're on the Nice list, Josh. Don't let him tell you otherwise," I said. Jillian buried her face in her hands.

"But what about the lying about my homework being done that I did yesterday?" he asked. "The mean Santa knew about it."

I glanced at my phone. "And then you confessed. Nice list, Josh, I promise." Then I crouched down and offered him my pinky. He solemnly completed the pinky promise.

My phone confirmed it—believer, top of the Nice list.

"Josh!" a voice called.

"I'm here, Mom! Bye, Santa's helper!" he said, throwing himself at me for a hug before dashing off.

Jillian tugged me into a corner. "I can't believe you did that! You can't stand here and try to fix every kid he talks to. We need to get his picture to Zen so the N-o-N can identify him."

Chastised, I ducked my head. "You're right. How do you want to do it?"

She led me to the line. "We'll get a picture with him. It can hang in a prominent place in your home."

I smirked, then leaned in to whisper into her ear. "As it happens, I have a picture of myself with Santa on my wall already." Jillian's lips twitched in response.

What I didn't have was a photo of the two of us. Just the two of us.

I watched carefully from our place in line and saw only one other child leave upset. It appeared whoever was behind the cloned phones was being slow and meticulous with the plan to destroy belief. But for the most part it was the standard I'd expected to find at a mall Santa set-up with the kids leaving happy and hopeful.

"Hi, ladies," the Santa greeted us when it was our turn. I handed my phone to the "elf" taking photos. I sat on Santa's left, and there, sticking out of the pocket of his coat was a Pole phone.

"Hi, Santa," we responded.

"So, what are you ladies hoping to receive for Christmas?" Santa asked us.

"I'm hoping for a new necklace," I used the euphemism for my sleigh harness I'd used before.

"And I'm thinking of a cashmere sweater," Jillian said.

"Well, if you've been good this year, I'm betting you'll find that under your tree." He chuckled as if he thought he was being very clever.

"Okay, can all three of you look at me?" The "elf" held up my phone and snapped a few photos.

"Nice to meet you, ladies," Santa said. "Merry Christmas!"

Much to my dismay, we were hurried out of his presence before I could do much of anything. I was worried the fake beard would impede it, but when I pulled up the photo on my phone, the N-o-N was able to identify him. Cameron Grey, twenty-seven, non-believer. Lifelong non-believer at that.

I sent the data to Zen and to Rudolph.

Turning to Jillian, I asked, "Now what should we do while we wait?"

"Times Square?" Jillian offered.

"Yes!"

After the masses in Macy's, we elected to walk to Times Square to avoid the crowds on the subway. While the city certainly wasn't quiet, it was still easier on the ears that the store had been. I reached for Jillian's hand and we walked side by side, only splitting up when the sidewalks got overly crowded. This part of Manhattan was easier to traverse than 5th Avenue, where people pressed their noses to the creative and unique holiday store windows, much as I had done on my first night in the city.

"Claudia? Are you still thinking about coming back after Christmas?" Jillian asked with a squeeze of my hand.

I looked at her. "If you're not sick of me."

She shook her head. "Not even a little. I'd love it if you came back."

"Do you get the six months after Christmas off, too?" Everyone at the Pole got six months of the year off, but it wasn't always the same six months depending on your department.

"I have to stick around for a few weeks after Christmas just to make sure all the i's are dotted and the t's are crossed, and that the skeleton crew that stays on from January until people return in July has what they need. But if you don't mind sticking around for that, we can stay here or go anywhere you want." Jillian squeezed my hand again.

"What if you get the job with Rudolph?"

"I'd report to the Pole in July instead of coming back to the City. I'm all yours for the first half of the year, though."

"I don't know what region I'll have next year." I said. "I should ask Wendy."

"Oh, I know where you'll be. Your next region is West North America, which includes Hawaii, if you want to find out what a beach getaway is like."

"Was that your plan?" I asked. "I don't want to make you stay in New York if you don't want to be here."

She tugged me until we were out of the line of foot traffic.

"I want to be with you," she said quietly. "I'm happy to be wherever you want to be. I had thought of going to Hawaii, but I didn't have any concrete plans."

She brushed some stray strands of hair out of my face and stole a kiss. Then her head turned and her brows drew down in a look of puzzlement. "Oh, my."

I turned to see that we were standing next to a window displaying many pairs of boots. Elf on the Shelf dolls popped up out of boots, sprawled over boots, and tobogganed down cotton batting between boots.

She continued on, having taken in the display. "I think the vision for this window was 'I meant to order one elf on the shelf for my kid but accidentally ordered one hundred.'"

"And I couldn't deal with the hassle of returning all the extras, so I'm using them in my window for the—? What do they call it on tv—?" I cast through my mind, searching through American media.

"For the effect?" Jillian suggested.

"For the tax write-off!" I crowed triumphantly.

Jillian's eyes got big, then she exploded in laughter. "For the tax—" Another burst of laughter interrupted her. After a moment she calmed, wiping at her eyes. "I'm crazy about you."

Two days ago, I couldn't have hoped for it. Today?

"I'm crazy about you, too." I went up on my toes and pressed a kiss to her cheek, her other cheek, her forehead, her nose, her jawline. When my lips finally captured hers, I was glad we were out of the pedestrian traffic. For several moments, the world melted away for one of Jillian's addictive kisses.

"You girls going to steam up my window or are you going to come buy some boots?" A voice sounded from the door of the store. We looked over and saw an amused septuagenarian with bright pink hair.

Why does it feel like every third person in New York has a fun hair color?

"Sorry, ma'am." I was mortified and my voice was full of contrition.

"Sorry, ma'am." Jillian echoed me. Her voice lacked any contrition—she was barely smothering a giggle as she turned tomato red.

The woman looked at Jillian. "I just bet you are. So sorry you'll be steaming up another window before you hit the next block."

Jillian's dimples showed themselves as she bit down on another laugh that escaped despite her best efforts. I coughed to try to disguise my own snort of laughter. My blush matched hers.

"You have the look of a troublemaker," the woman said to Jillian. She turned to me. "You'll have your hands full with her."

We dissolved into laughter. Her lips curved in magnanimous amusement.

We passed through the Garment District, and then the neon screens appeared, closer and closer. With every block a new sign came into my line of sight. Coke. *Wicked.* TKTS. The Marriott. On and on. In its own way, Times Square was as overwhelming as Macy's, but better because there was theater everywhere, and lots of open space, which kept the claustrophobia I had felt at Macy's at bay.

"I wish I could see this from up by where the ball drops," I said.

"You could always do it later tonight," Jillian suggested. "Or when you come back."

I met her eyes. "You could come with me. Have you ever ridden a reindeer?"

She shook her head, eyes wide. "Wouldn't that be a little unsafe?"

"No, they taught us how to in school," I told her. "I could carry you to up there and then we could look together."

"You're sweet to offer. I don't mind heights, but I need a solid floor under my feet and a barrier between me and falling. And I need to travel via elevator. I trust you, but I'm too scared that I might fall." Jillian said.

I nodded. "Then I can take pictures for you instead."

"That sounds excellent."

We walked around for about a half hour. I stared at the TKTS offerings and decided which show I would go see that night if things were different—*The Phantom of the Opera*. Then we sat down at a stray table with two chairs near TKTS to eat pretzels, which I learned to eat with mustard. Jillian took my picture so I could show my mom and my friends.

"I have pictures of us with the Sugar Plum Fairy and with a faux Santa, but none of just us." I remarked, glancing at the photo of us from Macy's before sending it to Jillian.

"We should take some selfies!"

Jillian fished out her phone. She flicked the camera to front facing. I leaned in and Jillian started taking photos.

"How do you want to pose? Let's do a fun one—silly faces!" I suggested.

"Now serious faces," Jillian said, pulling her eyebrows down in a mockery of a serious face. I snorted and tried to look down my nose at the camera.

Once we stopped giggling, we started trying to top each other for the most ludicrous suggestions.

"Famous people tired of the paparazzi?"

"Chefs who don't approve of this last bite of pretzel."

"Tourists who are confused by Times Square."

"So hungry we're planning a heist of the M&M store."

At that I burst out laughing. "Yes, that's us—career criminals."

"Here's one we haven't done—kiss me."

"Gladly." And several moments later, I said, "I want copies of all of those."

"Of course!"

When I checked my phone to see the pictures downloading from Jillian, there was an email alert. "Oh! Jillian, we need to go back to the apartment. They're sending us security."

She frowned. "Security?"

I leaned in and whispered in her ear. "A snowman."

She raised an eyebrow. "Here? But—"

"It'll be fine," I reassured her.

Snowmen are blue—blue hair, blue eyes, blue skin. I could see her reason for concern—a blue person would stand out, even on the streets of New York. But I'd done research on snowmen for one of my classes on people at the Pole and adaptations of each species. We spent about seventy-five percent of the class learning about elves and the various jobs they did and how it related back to our role as a team member. But I'd found snowmen fascinating, especially as I hadn't really interacted with any at that point in my life. What I'd learned is that some snowmen are capable of changing their skin color—it took tremendous effort, but there was a small percentage who knew how to do it.

When we got back to HQ, we found the snowman waiting for us.

"Kyle." He thrust out his hand to each of us in turn and we shook it.

He was a head and a half taller than me, and very muscular. And clearly he was one of the few who could change his color. Now that he wasn't blue, he looked like club bouncers I'd seen in movies. His skin was a pale white, his hair was black with a slight blueish sheen, and his eyes were still a piercing Artic blue. "We know his address. When the phone shows he's at home, we're going to go over and talk to him with the goal of getting it back and finding out as much as we can. We want to know how he got his hands on a Pole phone. Claudia, you're still point person—this is your mission."

We surveilled Cameron's phone, and at seven-thirty p.m. he left Macy's. By nine-thirty the phone was in his apartment.

"It's go time." Kyle stood and cracked his neck.

At Cameron's apartment building, we had the good luck to arrive at the same time as someone else. They let us inside. Cameron lived in an older building without a doorman, so we were able to walk up to the fifth floor unimpeded.

In front of Cameron's door, I exchanged a look with Kyle and Jillian, swallowed, shoving my anxiety—which currently had my stomach in my throat—down as far as I could make it go. It was still a constant niggling in my mind. Waving my hand, I gestured for them to step out of the line of sight. My hand lifted, I took a deep breath, and then I let it knock three times.

The door opened, and Cameron was there. He was around Kyle's height, but with a slighter build. I wouldn't have recognized him without the Santa gear if my phone hadn't shown me a picture of him in street clothes. He looked me over and frowned.

"Can I help you?"

"Hi, Cameron. I think you have something of mine."

No point in being coy. We had discussed several other scenarios, but they all seemed like a waste of time. And now that we were face to face, it turned out I was infuriated by his successful destruction of belief, so I wasn't interested in playing games.

He frowned, but laughed. "You look familiar."

"Invite me in," I said.

"I like a woman who knows what she wants. But I'm not exactly prepared for visitors," he said with a shrug. "So don't complain."

I moved forward and Kyle and Jillian stepped up behind me.

"Hey, what is this?" Cameron demanded, trying to push the door closed.

Kyle held the door open with one hand.

"Hey, let it go. What's wrong with you? What is this?" Cameron was shoving at the door, but Kyle didn't even look like he was exerting much strength to hold it.

"This is about your magic phone, Cameron. You're not supposed to have that," I said.

He froze, and we were able to push past him, Kyle kicking the door closed behind us. Cameron was still looking at me slack-jawed.

"Give me the phone, Cameron," I ordered, my voice more commanding than I'd ever heard it before.

"I don't know what you're talking about!" he shouted.

"Lying isn't going to help your case, Cameron," Jillian said.

"I saw it in your pocket at Macy's," I added. "And I know for a fact that it's here right now."

"How could you know that?"

"Because you're not on the Nice list, Cameron. You stole a Pole phone and you've been using it to ruin people's belief in Santa and Christmas magic," I said taking an angry step toward him. He took a step back.

"I didn't steal anything! Who are you?" His voice was getting high pitched with fear.

"Why would you hurt kids, Cameron?" Kyle asked. "They're kids."

Cameron slumped. "It's kinda mean to do, I know. But it's only a few more weeks. I promised ten kids a day."

"Why?" The question flew from my lips unprompted. "And promised who?"

"This guy is going to pay off my student loans if I do this. And look, it's not like any of this stuff is real. Santa and all that—I grew up just fine without it. They might cry for a few days, but once they get over it, they'll see that it was all a bunch of BS." Cameron said.

"So if Santa is fake, then the ends justifies the means?" I asked.

He is on my last freaking nerve.

"Yes. I'm not saying it's the choice everyone would make, but those loans are a beast. I still owe ten years of payments on them."

"What if Santa is real?" I asked.

"What?"

"If Santa is fake then the ends justifies the means, and it's no harm, no foul. But what if Santa is real?" Jillian said, seeing where I was going.

"You want me to play pretend?" Cameron's earlier fear was giving way to annoyance. "Look, you people are nuts. Get out of my apartment or I'll call the cops."

We hadn't planned for this. But I felt like it was the right approach. "Who said I'm pretending?"

He crossed his arms. "Get out."

I took a few judicious steps forward and morphed. Cameron screamed and fell down as he backed away from me. I put a hoof on his ankle.

"I'd give her the phone," Kyle said.

"You an elf or something?" he asked, his voice wavering.

Kyle released his hold on his skin color, and he was suddenly a very beautiful light blue. "Snowman."

Jillian stepped forward with a wave. "Hi. I'm the elf. I don't do any cool magic—I'm an administrator."

I morphed back to human form and held out my hand. "Give me the phone, Cameron."

He got to his feet and walked to his kitchen, where it was charging on the counter. "Please don't hurt me," he whispered.

I snatched the phone when he went to put it in my palm. "Now answer Kyle's questions."

"I'll get in trouble," Cameron said.

"Cameron, how do you think your neighbors will react when I shift and start clip clopping all over their ceiling? My antlers could knock over a lot of things because I'm clumsy in my reindeer form. You don't want me to do that, do you?" I held out my hand and morphed it to my hoof, then released it. It was painful to do a partial shift, and I could only hold it for a few moments, but it was enough to make my point.

"Fine."

Jillian and I watched as Kyle questioned Cameron.

"How do you communicate with—" his voice trailed off expectantly.

"Mr. der Bock. His number is programmed into the phone. I text him how many believers I take off the list, and he transfers money into my bank account each night. Like today there were eleven, so I texted him after work and came home." Cameron sat on a chair and held his head in his hands. "It's all— You're real."

He glanced at his coffee table.

"I must be baked."

"Did you smoke since getting home?" Jillian asked.

"N-no, but I *have* to be high." He insisted.

"When did der Bock approach you?" Kyle asked.

"A week ago."

"How?"

"This guy I know from grad school? Travis? He said it was just a way to make some extra money and no one would ever know. A hundred dollars for every person who gave up on believing in Santa. So, I said yes, and he hooked me up with der Bock. I only met him once to get the phone and everything. Since then, I've only ever talked to der Bock over text or voice call. I didn't think you were —" Cameron said before I cut him off.

"Here's the thing, Cameron. It doesn't matter if we're real. You screwed with kids' belief systems. You told them they were *bad*. You abused the database we set up to track Nice and Naughty acts, zeroing in on one thing or another, when it's the whole person we look at. You broke children's —and some adult's—hearts," I said, my voice going harsh. "You need to make up for that."

His eyes met mine. "What do you want me to do?"

"You're going to quit your job, but you're going to recommend the person we tell you to recommend for Macy's," I said. "You won't contact Mr. der Bock."

"I won't. I was going to move after the holidays," he said. "My lease is up on January first. I can leave sooner."

"Fine. Promise you'll never try to be a Santa again."

"No offense, but I wasn't the hugest fan of kids before now, and I'm definitely not a fan now that I've been Santa for a few weeks. I've been peed on and sneezed on and whined at and kicked—I won't do it again."

"Good. Now answer Kyle's questions." Due to his imposing size, Kyle was the best person to intimidate Cameron into answering our questions. I'd told Kyle what I was thinking we should ask, but that he should use his judgment. Sometimes the best choice was to delegate.

Kyle spent an hour grilling Cameron on everything from his communications with der Bock—their first meeting, every text message, his methods— to der Bock's appearance and mannerisms.

"Keep your word on everything you've promised. Because we'll be keeping an eye on you, Cameron," Kyle said.

And with that, we left.

Once back at headquarters, Kyle used the transporter and took the illicit phone to Zen before returning to the Pole. Jillian and I didn't watch *The Devil Wears Prada*, but I did hear Meryl Streep being haughty in the background while I kissed Jillian until my lips were swollen.

Chapter Eight

In the morning, an email arrived from Rudolph. She wanted all of the reindeer to practice flying the new routes she'd designed for all the regions, then get to the Pole by nightfall. During the official flight, I'd be yoked behind Rudolph. My job was to memorize the location of each and every individual house in my region, and Rudolph trusted me to keep her on track. She knew the flight plan, but not every single house we delivered to in every single area—even just the top percentage of the Nice list equated to over a million gifts.

I felt like my stomach was doing the mambo. Had I done enough? Was I going to be allowed to fly next year, or would they replace me? When I asked myself why I wouldn't be allowed to fly next year, I couldn't come up with anything rational or plausible. But *Stealing a phone is a Naughty list move!* played on repeat in my brain. So did *You morphed in front of a human!* and *You told a child they were on the Nice list!* As far as my fears could tell, I might have screwed up so much that they wouldn't let me leave the Pole ever again.

I needed to consume a big breakfast to fuel my flight, so Jillian brought me to a diner. It wasn't quite like in the movies, but the food was delicious and there was a lot of it.

"Can I call you while you're gone?" Jillian asked, playing with her New York Rangers beanie. "Or will you be too busy? The Big Show is your priority right now."

With a rush, my anxiety, which had been quiet, roared back to life. I swallowed it down, reached out and took her hand. When her eyes met mine, I said, "Please call me. I might answer at odd times, or not be able to talk for long, but you're important to me."

Will you want to date me if I'm trapped at the Pole?

She flashed her dimples. "I hope you know you're important to me, too. I'm looking forward to spending time with you after you get back."

"What about the job with Rudolph?" Maybe that would make living back at the Pole bearable. *She* would be based out of the Pole six months a year.

"With the attack on Christmas, the application process stalled. I think once there's some kind of resolution, we'll go back to interviewing."

I told my anxious brain to shut up and tried to make normal conversation. "I'm thinking that maybe we stay in New York until you're done, then head to Hawaii so you can get that beach vacation. Then we can bop around Western North America? I'd like to take some time to get to know all the parts of that region."

"Sounds perfect. Guess I need to go swimwear shopping." She grinned mischievously.

The mental images scrambled my brains, and I realized I was staring at her like a starving woman. I blurted out the first thing that crossed my mind. "Don't you sunburn?" I had no idea. For that matter, I didn't know if *I* sunburned. I filed that away to ask Wendy.

"That's what waterproof sunscreen is for," she said with a smile. "And having to help me apply it? I don't know, seems like it will be kind of a trial for you."

"I mean, if I *have* to." I shivered with delight at the idea of her rubbing lotion on me in turn.

She laughed. "I've never seen a reindeer's home, and I'd like to see yours at the Pole sometime. You can give me the big tour. Maybe when I interview with Rudolph."

"Absolutely."

Since that's where I'll be trapped.

"Is the food okay?" Jillian bit her lip. "I should've taken you downtown to my favorite diner instead of finding one near the building. Sorry. It was well reviewed on Yelp."

"The food is fine," I said, and shoveled some egg into my mouth. "I just have a lot on my mind."

I managed to eat enough to keep Jillian from worrying about my upcoming flight, but after a certain point, I was just forcing myself to eat. The eggs formed a leaden lump in my stomach, which just made me more uncomfortable. But the longer we sat there, the more my anxiety crept up on me, threatening to reduce me to a mass of trembling Christmas jelly.

At the apartment, I packed up the little souvenirs I'd saved or purchased to be transported back. I passed the box to Jillian, then burst into tears.

"Claudia!" She put the box on the couch and pulled me into her embrace, and I clutched at her. "Oh, hey, what brought this on?"

It all poured out. All my anxiety. All my fears. "—and I morphed, Jillian, in front of a *human*. They're going to punish me! Why did I do that?" My breathing was getting faster and faster until I was at risk of falling into a whirlpool of thoughts and negative feelings.

"Hold on, wait a second. Breathe... Now, how can I help you?"

I nodded, Jillian's words reminding me to remember the mnemonic. "I'm— I can't— Ok, I'm going to do a thing to calm down and center myself."

How did it go again? S.T.O.P

Stop and pause. Stop. Pause. I don't have to go anywhere in this second. I don't have to do anything. I can pause and...

Take a breath. I inhaled deeply and slowly let the breath hiss out. I did it three times.

Observe what's happening in my body. It felt like my ribs were being squeezed, and my stomach had fish flopping in it.

Proceed with awareness. Once I named those sensations, I could control them enough to let them recede until they were bearable. I reminded myself that nothing was actually constricting my ribs, and took several deep breaths to prove it. I quieted the fish until they were just butterflies.

"Sorry, I totally freaked out on you." I chewed on my lower lip as I looked at Jillian.

"You told me you get panic attacks. It's okay," she said. "Do you have time to cuddle on the couch for like half an hour? We can put on something stupid and just breathe calmly or something?"

The second she suggested it, I felt lighter. My body was telling me I needed it—whether for anxiety or for personal reasons, or a mixture of the two. "Yes, let's do that."

I spent a half hour in her arms, my head on her shoulder while something played on television. When it was over, Jillian walked me to the roof. Her blue eyes were sad when we reached the door.

"I'm going to miss you, Claudia," she said. Her thumb ghosted along my cheek.

"I'm going to miss *you*," I replied.

Our kiss started gentle, but quickly became a conflagration. I couldn't get enough of Jillian. It was as if I could more eloquently express myself with my lips than my words. She kissed me just as desperately, intent on possessing each other. When we broke apart, we were both breathing more harshly than I had when I was catastrophizing.

"I hate leaving you. But I'll see you in a few weeks," I said to Jillian.

"I'm going to miss you so much. Call me when you arrive at the Pole, please. To let me know you got home safe?"

"Of course. It's going to be really late though."

"You're right." Jillian twisted her lips into that face she made when thinking. "Well, maybe at least text me before you fall asleep, so I don't worry, okay?"

"Deal."

I put up my sight shield, morphed and I was off. I did the full route, and this close to Christmas, there was so much magic that I wasn't even tired. I got a little freaked by the air traffic near some of the big hubs, like Atlanta, but I calculated the right height at which to fly. I may have circled the castle at Disney World more than once, and I may have landed on the Epcot dome to take a picture to send to Jillian while in Orlando. I completed the final leg and when I reached the designated spot where I'd pass the sleigh off to the next reindeer, I headed north to the Pole.

Breaking through the barrier to the Pole was bittersweet. I was glad to be home, but part of me was certain that my freedom was over.

When I landed at the runway, there were a few calves watching.

"Are you Comet?" one of them yelled.

"Yes," I replied. *For now.*

"Can I have your autograph?"

"Me too?"

They wanted my autograph? My first thought was *I'm not a real team member*. But no, I *was* a real team member. I had completed a mission from Rudolph, and successfully. Jillian and I had been a good team. I approached the fence.

"I'm Elanor," one said.

"I'm Rhi," the other said.

"My mom said you were asked to pull the sleigh on like December first. Was it scary?"

I whuffed at the calf. "A little bit."

"Is it super awesome, to fly out there?"

"The most awesome," I replied with a grin.

I signed their autograph books.

This time I was confident when I gave my hoofprint to get into the barn.

"Go on, Comet," the snowman said to me.

Once in the barn, I texted Jillian then sought out Rudolph. I had to know how much trouble I was in. How many of my fears were real and how many were just my anxiety lying to me.

"Good, you're here," Rudolph said. She tossed her red hair over her shoulder. "We can get this over with. You're confined to the Pole for two weeks because of the whole morphing in front of a human thing. Effective immediately. So, until the Big Show. Except for team practices."

I started to object that team practices were daily events. Then I thought it through. You have to stay at the Pole until you're scheduled to go on vacation, except for daily practices. Basically, she was ordering me to do what I had to do anyway. That had to be intentional. I hid a smile, realizing that while Rudolph couldn't officially say it was fine—it would set a bad precedent—she had chosen to make my punishment a "punishment."

"Apart from that, you should give yourself and Jillian huge kudos for your mission. You recovered both phones, and we have been able to use some of Cameron's data to try to find out more about his contact."

"Thank you," I answered.

"You'll want to move your stuff into the barn until the Big Show. These last few weeks are a whirlwind." Rudolph said.

She wasn't exaggerating. The last two weeks leading up to the Big Show were jam packed. The cloned Pole phones had all gone dark a day after we'd recovered Cameron's phone. Whether that was because Cameron had told on us or because der Bock had learned of the events of the week, I didn't know.

The team had important priorities, though, that had nothing to do with der Bock. Each day during our countdown to the Big Show we'd practice flying a region. The team had actually reported back sixteen days before the Big Show so that we could fly each of the eight routes two times. For those sixteen days, first thing in the morning we'd fly the designated route, then we'd repeat it twice more. During lunch we'd sit around and debate about how it could've gone smoother. In the afternoon, we'd fly it twice more. Over dinner we'd discuss the afternoon and compare it to the morning. I didn't have energy to stay awake much past dinner.

Throughout it all, the other reindeer gradually pulled me out of my shell. Zen made the biggest effort—she'd been really touched by the ornament, and had made it her mission to make me feel included. When Caity noticed, she joined in and also made a point of asking me for my thoughts. When the subject inevitably changed to our lives,

I gradually shared about my life. They loved the stories of how I recovered the phones. I heard about Caity's Iron Man competitions and her try at the Boston Marathon this year. Cupid told us some of the more choice anecdotes about her students. Vixen lived up to her name and laughed about her conquests. Each day I felt closer to belonging, until by the twenty-third I felt like part of the cohesive unit.

The upside of this was that we always stopped for food in one of the regions. We ate bao in China, lamb in Australia, jollof rice in Nigeria, poutine in Canada, and more. We even stopped for part of a k-pop concert for Dancer's birthday, because Dancer "needed a rest," so we watched for an hour. (Turns out I'm a Blackpink fan.)

The downside was that my days were busier than I'd ever dreamt of being. I felt bad because I couldn't call Jillian at a time she was around very often. I emailed her back, I texted, I sent memes and gifs, but I worried that it was too little.

Finally, it was the night I'd dreamed of my whole life. The Big Show.

Wendy came to the barn in human form to see us off.

"Claudia, I'm so proud of you. You'll do amazing," she said, helping an elf fasten my harness.

"She's a worthy Comet. I think you should be worried, Wendy," Zen said as she was harnessed next to me.

"Oh, I have a feeling that things will work out just fine for everyone," she said confidently.

"Wendy isn't the only one who should be worried. Comet is the one who used a kid—" Prancer—Caity—began.

"That was all Jillian's idea," I interrupted.

"—used a kid," she repeated "and she's the one who got her phones. Our biggest lead in this whole mess came from Comet. If Wendy wants to come back, I'm worried about *my* job security because I don't want us to lose Claudia."

I was glad to be in my reindeer form because I could feel my whole head burning, not just my face. "Guys. I'm happy to help out."

"Tell us again how you made the human pee his pants when you morphed," Vixen said—I could hear the smirk in her voice.

I laughed and rolled my eyes. "I told you that's an exaggeration. He didn't pee his pants."

There were several snorts of amusement.

Then it was time to fly.

Words are not adequate to describe that night. Exhilaration sang through my veins—I was doing it! I was living my dream! Racing the clock definitely had me worried, but as long as Zen and the others were calm, I was able to keep calm as well.

When we hit the headquarters of each region, the elves were ready with snacks and water for us. Santa was fueled by the cookies and treats of the believers, but not everyone thought of us, and not every region had a tradition of treats for the reindeer. So the elves ensured that the team was well cared for.

"Claudia, which one are you?" Lee asked when we landed in New York. Jillian had told me in an email that she had given Lee permission to help with feeding and watering the team. As far as Lee was concerned, greeting the team was her present for being on the Nice list.

"Here I am!" I called out.

Lee and Jillian hurried over to me, while other elves helped my teammates. Lee scratched between my ears and offered me some sweet-smelling hay. Jillian had water.

"I've missed you both," I said, although I only had eyes for Jillian.

"We miss you, too," Jillian said. She petted my muzzle, then leaned to my ear so that only I would hear her. "I especially miss kissing you."

I swallowed. "Me, too."

"Then I hope you're ready to have your socks kissed off when you get back," she murmured.

"Five-minute warning!" Santa called out. He tapped on the screen mounted in front of him. "Jubilee, come here please."

I whuffed with pleasure. I didn't know what Santa had gotten her.

"Yes, Santa?"

"Your help was instrumental in investigating the people trying to kill belief. I want you to know how what a difference your help made. Without your lead, we might not have been able to stop the bad Santas. I hope you like your present. It's a little heavy, though. Jillian, why don't you help her?" He handed Jillian a wrapped gift. "You can open it, Lee. Ah, Ah," he raised a finger to quiet Lee when she'd opened her mouth in protestation. "You deserve it. Take it with the gratitude of the Pole."

Lee threw herself at Santa and hugged him. I smiled indulgently—she was such a good kid. Santa gave her one of his big bear hugs. I remembered his hugs from my childhood. They were amazing and made you feel protected from anything bad that could possibly happen.

She tore at the wrapping paper and gasped. "A sewing machine, just for me?"

"I know your sewing lessons have been going well, so it's time."

"*Thank you*, Santa!"

"You're very welcome, Jubilee. Jillian, you're top of the Nice list, too—"

Jillian ducked her head. "Thanks, Santa."

"—and here are tickets to *Six, Hamilton,* and *Mean Girls* for you and a friend. Please accept them with the gratitude of the Pole as well. Good work—you and Comet make a good team."

"We do," Jillian said with a glance in my direction.

"Merry Christmas! Okay, everyone, *to the top of the porch! To the top of the wall! Now dash away, dash away, dash away all!*"

Jillian had said I'd be alert through the whole flight, but I was running on fumes by the end. When we arrived at the final headquarters, I was so tired I wanted to lie down.

"You have to eat something," Zen urged me.

"I'm so tired," I whined.

"The first time is brutal," Vixen said. "Don't you remember, Zen? Comet, you have to eat to get that last bit of energy. There's only a little more, then we hit the islands and we're done. Next year it will feel so much easier, I swear."

With their encouragement, I ate. They were right that I did feel a *little* better once I had.

It was like flying through wet cement for the last hour, even though the sleigh was empty. As we got closer to the Pole, I was worried I might crash instead of landing. But as we came in for our final approach, I was grateful for all our practices because muscle memory took over, and I helped land the sleigh smoothly to the cheers of the waiting crowd.

"Tomorrow, we have a full team meeting with P.A.s to discuss what we've learned about the attack on Christmas," Santa announced. "Please wait to leave until after the meeting."

I hung my head and tried to stay awake while we were

unbuckled. I heard murmurs from the team and the elves helping us out of our harnesses, but I was too tired to try to parse any of it.

Zen walked me to my stall. I was weaving a bit. "All joking aside, you are no longer Kid Comet—you're just Comet. Way to go, Claudia."

"What happened to names are for away from the barn?" I joked wearily when we got to my stall.

Zen shook her head. "Meh. You earned it."

I stumbled inside and fell asleep on the hay.

Thirty or so hours later, a knock at the door woke me. Muttering about coffee, I lifted my head and blinked several times. Adrenaline surged through my body at the sight of Jillian at my door. I morphed into human form and threw myself at her.

Several moments later, I exclaimed, "You're here!" I looked her up and down. "You're so fancy." She wore a silky gold top under a tailored light gray pantsuit.

"I just had my interview with Rudolph, and I have to attend the meeting. As a bonus, I get to see you," she said. "It was so cool seeing you flying the sleigh during the Big Show. You must be really proud! I know I'm proud of you."

"I am. But I'm betting my mother is bragging to every person she meets that her baby helped pull the sleigh. She's probably prouder than both of us put together!"

Jillian's lips quirked. "Sounds like she'd get along with my mother, who makes sure that people know her baby is a P.A."

The meeting was a virtual Who's Who of important elves, snowmen, and reindeer. There were about ten minutes before the meeting was scheduled to start, and Jillian and I sat near the front watching people filter in. I recognized Kyle, who gave us a wave. Cupid sat down a few seats away and pulled a book out of her bag. Donner slouched next to her and said something to Cupid that made her roll her eyes, and give Donner a look with one eyebrow arched before going back to her book. Wendy came in with Zen, their heads bent together. Rudolph appeared with the Clauses. Jillian waved at several gold-clad elves—some of the other P.A.s—but she made no move to leave my side.

Santa stood at the front of the room and clapped his hands. He'd trimmed his beard from big and bushy to trimmed and neat. He wore a white button-up shirt and black slacks. Mrs. Claus stood beside him wearing a white dress. They wouldn't look out of place at a board meeting of a Fortune 500 company. Reindeer didn't have a designated color so I'd gone for an evergreen dress. The room quickly grew silent. "As you know, we experienced a breach of security."

Zen buried her head in her hands and Wendy rubbed her back. Her life's work was being used against the Pole, and she was clearly devastated.

"A Pole phone was acquired one way or another, and then cloned. The clones were distributed with the intention of ruining belief."

I flashed back to my conversations with the adults, and what Lee had told me the kids were saying, to the little boy at Macy's. They had been successful. More than fifty lost believers in New York. It would've been more, too, if we hadn't been able to acquire the phones.

"The phones were abruptly shut off the morning after Comet's team acquired the second phone and a name. Blitzen is putting in new safeguards, and you will all be given new logins for the N-o-N once she's finished."

Zen looked so frustrated, I wanted to go hug her. Wendy was on top of it, though, and was hugging Zen from one side. An elf I didn't recognize hugged her from the other. Vixen was behind her and rested her hands comfortingly on Zen's shoulders.

"Kyle investigated the man who contacted and manipulated the humans. His name is der Bock. He is, from what we can tell, a wealthy human who made an obscene amount of money in technology—which is likely how he was able to hack and then clone Pole phones."

"But how could a human break into the N-o-N?" Wei Liang protested. "And what's to stop him from doing it again?"

"Now that I know, I've been able to neutralize external access to the N-o-N. He won't get us that way again," Zen said.

"What's his N-o-N history?" Wendy interjected.

"We can't find him under the name Karl der Bock, although that's the name in news articles about him. He's reclusive—we couldn't find a picture of him. Without a photo, we really don't have much to go on. Cameron described der Bock, and our artists have created a sketch, but it produced too many results to get a clear N-o-N identification or history." Santa's displeasure at that was palpable.

"But he'll probably come after us again in a different way, won't he?" Donner's voice was skeptical.

Santa affirmed that fear. "We don't know where he is or what his agenda is, but we have to assume this was not a one-time-only assault on belief. We want you to go on vacation as planned, but keep an eye out for anything that seems fishy. We're distributing sketches of der Bock. If you see him, do not approach. Reach out to the Pole. Be careful."

Jillian and I nodded.

"And on that note, enjoy your vacation."

Jillian followed me to my home. I had to pack what I wanted for the next six months. I could always come back if I forgot something, but I was looking forward to my time away from the Pole. She looked around my little home with interest.

"Sorry, it doesn't have a lot of human accoutrements. Just what I need to study and to practice human things." I said, a little unsure of what she'd think. I had a coffee maker, but not a stove. I had a bathroom, but not a bedroom. There was no kitchen for us to make pancakes. "I'm getting a house barn when we come back in July because I'm a team member. I thought I wouldn't, since I'm temporary, but they told me that I'd earned it. Maybe you can help me with decorating it. I liked the apartment in New York."

"I'd love to help. Is that you and your mom?" she asked pointing at a picture.

"Yes. She's really nice, but you don't have to meet her today," I said with a smile. "I told her goodbye already." I put the picture of myself and my mother in the box along with some books and cables. We walked to the barn, where I packed up my laptop.

Jillian and I went to the transporter room where we were sent back to New York. It was just as unpleasant as before. The lurching in my stomach was awful, but bearable. But that itching—like a thousand mosquito bites demanding to be scratched—remained one of the most uncomfortable experiences of my life.

Next time I'll fly rather than be transported.

We used the theater tickets, and I was thrilled to be in the audience of a Broadway show. *Nutcracker* had been magical, but *this* was what I'd dreamed of. After seeing *Six*, I begged Jillian to go to the stage door with me so I could get the cast's autographs. She smiled in amusement, her dimples winking at me. It was a long wait to meet all of the queens, but I was able to send a fully autographed poster back to the Pole to be framed and placed on my wall.

The elves asked to photograph me for the official apartment picture. I was relieved when the print didn't reveal my blushing cheeks.

It turned out that there was something better than going to Times Square to see the ball drop on New Year's Eve, and that was spending it with Jillian. I had trouble keeping my mind on the countdown show that Jillian had put on.

Jillian was humming along with a band I was unfamiliar with when I found my courage.

"Jillian? There's something I've been wanting to tell you," I confessed. I chewed on my lower lip.

"This sounds serious. What is it, sweetheart?" Jillian's fingers were feather light as they brushed over my cheekbone. She muted the television and gave me her full attention.

"I'm falling for you." I blurted it out.

Her eyes widened, and then she gave me a dazzling smile and said, "I've been wanting to tell you the same."

We started kissing, even though it was five minutes from midnight. Things were heating up by the time the crowd on television counted down to zero. How else to ensure a good year to come?

❄

Six weeks later

When Caity heard we were going to Hawaii, she'd insisted we should try paddle boarding. So this morning, we'd rented some boards and off we'd gone. Jillian tumbled from the board several times before finding her balance, but to my surprise, I took to it quickly. After a pleasant afternoon and lovely dinner at the hotel restaurant overlooking the ocean, we retired to the suite. My hand drifted over my stomach, where my muscles were feeling the effects of my tensing them while I'd balanced.

"Sore from the paddle boarding?" Jillian asked.

"It was so much fun," I said. "What should we try tomorrow?"

"Maybe we should try surfing. And you want to go on a Whale Watch, right?" Her phone chirped, and Jillian absently picked it up to see the cause.

"Yes, I really want to—" I started to speak but Jillian inhaled sharply.

She sat up at attention. "Claudia, the email from Rudolph is here. I can't open it." She closed her eyes and held her phone close to her chest. "Just breathe. I didn't get it. I know I didn't get the job. Gemma is more experienced—she'll have gotten it," Jillian muttered. She turned the phone over and over in her hands. It was shocking to see her normally unflappable self ruffled. "I'm scared to open an email. This ridiculous. Ugh!" She put the phone down and glared at it.

I offered my hand. "Can I help?"

"Yes," she said, and took my hand. "Okay. I'm going to open it. Don't be disapp—" Jillian stopped.

"Jillian?"

She stared at her phone. "Claudia?"

"Jillian?"

"I sure hope you meant it when you said you'd help me adjust to life at the Pole." She gave me a smile that rocked me to my core. "I got it. IgotitIgotitIgotit!" Her excited grin brightened the whole room!

I whooped and tackled her in a hug.

Best. Holiday. Season. Ever.

Acknowledgments

Thank you for reading Comet's First Christmas. I had no clue when 2020 began that I'd finish it with a gentle holiday novella. The idea for Comet was born in 2016 as an erotic short story. However, when I decided she deserved a longer story, I found she'd changed in the last four years, and I no longer wanted to write that iteration. But after how bruising 2020 has been, can anyone blame us for wanting something a little sweet?

I decided to write a character with anxiety because it is something I've been living with for a long time. Claudia manages it using techniques that have been extremely helpful to me. However, unlike Comet, I also use medication to manage the anxiety.

I lived in New York in 2002 while I was attending NYU for exactly one semester. I loved the city, my job working for a Broadway ticket discounter, and the friends I made. I did not love NYU, and I only needed one semester to tell me that my graduate program had been a mistake. *But* living there over one Christmas season, I fell in love. This book let me revisit all those NYC memories from when I was twenty-three.

This marks my second full-length book, and my first queer book. As a queer woman who is married to a man, I've dealt with a lot of imposter syndrome over the years about what stories I'm queer "enough" to write, and it's taken me a lot of time to get to this place.

There are tons of people to thank for this book, but I want to focus on five. My writing partner, Johanna, who kept me motivated and believed in me when I was panic-texting her at one a.m. My editor, Jessica, whose support over the past seven years has helped me grow tremendously. My family—Ravi, Rhi, and Elanor—gave me tons of support, room to write, and let me babble on about my book at great length. Elanor gets her own shout-out, though, for telling me to make all nine reindeer lesbians.

Read on for the first chapter of Zen's Second Chance
Releasing 10/19/21

If you enjoyed Comet's First Christmas, please consider leaving a review.

Join my mailing list to hear about new releases. I write a variety of pairing and heat levels—if you join, you'll be able to keep up on my releases.

For other stories I've written, I have a breakdown of them based on pairing and heat level here.

Excerpt from Zen's Second Chance

ZEN

It was all my fault.

I rubbed a hand over the back of my neck as I watched the coffee maker refill my cup for the sixth time today. I was probably giving myself an ulcer, but until I finished adding another layer of security on the Pole's technology, I wouldn't be able to eat, sleep, or even come close to functioning normally. I looked at my bowl of moss, completely untouched, and shrugged. Coffee was enough fuel for this reindeer.

Three weeks ago, I'd been alerted to a precipitous drop off in Santa Claus believers. After some investigating, we learned that some tech billionaire named der Bock had breached my security on the Naughty-or-Nice database. He then hired people around the world to target top nice believers and paid them per person they managed to convince to stop believing in Santa.

And he'd used technology I invented to do it.

Turning regular phones into specialized phones with two modes—normal and Pole—had been an early idea of mine that had only gotten more and more popular. Until der Bock somehow obtained a Pole phone and used it against us.

How many of my other "revolutionary" ideas will come back to bite me on the butt?

I watched my code critically, looking for any weakness that could be exploited.

"You're *still* here? Zen, it's January third." Rudolph stuck her head through the door of my stall/office in Reindeer Complex. Her waterfall of auburn hair streamed down over her back to touch her hips. I used to love braiding it as a little girl, back when she was just Rose, and not Rudolph. She'd joined the team as Prancer when I was in middle school and had been promoted to Rudolph six years ago.

"Yeah, I'm still anxious about leaving. Maybe I should just stay at the Pole this year," I said, eyes glued to the code.

"Do you not have employees, Zen? We've talked about work/life balance in the past. You can delegate work," Rudolph sat in the chair facing my desk. Clearly this was going to be a longer than usual visit. "You know the reason we take six months off is because we *have* to. That's why we slow down so much when we fly after the Big Show. Christmas Eve takes *everything* out of you. For your magic to replenish, you need to actually *relax*. Go to a nerdy convention or something."

"I can't delegate work if I can't anticipate when or how the system will be attacked." I tried to keep my creeping irritation in check. I felt like my teeth might shatter at any second from being clenched. I just wanted to do my job.

"It's my fault December happened. I'm going to ensure it doesn't happen again."

"Persephone. None of us are psychic. It's impossible to anticipate anything a madman will do. Have your employees watch your servers in shifts so you'll know immediately if they're breached. I'm really worried about you. You're drowning yourself in guilt for something that wasn't your fault." Rudolph used a soothing tone that had the opposite effect on me.

I let out a little hiss of annoyance. When she looked at me, I met her concerned gaze and snapped, "I'm fine."

"You're not fine, Percy." Using my special nickname was a low blow and I scowled. She'd been my baby-sitter when I was little, and she got Percy privileges along with my parents and close friends—to everyone else at the Pole I was Zen or Blitzen. My job title was preferable to Persephone. In the human world, however, Percy got me fewer odd looks than introducing myself as Zen.

I knew she was right.

"Okay, maybe I'm working towards fine, *Rose*. But I'll get there a lot faster if you just let me do this—" I gestured to the computer screen. "*There you are.*" I growled at the bug I'd been looking for for the past three hours. Okay, so maybe it wasn't guilt so much as it was feeling like I wasn't in charge, wasn't in control of the situation. But if I just sat here long enough, I could prevent a breach from ever occurring again.

"Percy."

I held up one finger then bent my head to type furiously. I was going to squash this little jerk and then I was going to find the next one. And the next. And the next.

"Percy."

"Gimmeaminute," I muttered, fingers flying over the keys

"Persephone, you need to go somewhere that isn't here."

"Can't. Talk. Coding," I bit out.

Rudolph threw up her hands and walked out of my office. I'd have to suck up to her later—show up at her office with candy cane coffee or something. But really, I was better off by myself with the code.

Things went peacefully for another two hours. I found and eliminated two more bugs. When I was satisfied, I sent the code to my head elf at the Pole, Liam. *Have five different elves do code review on this.* Five should be enough.

As I got up to get coffee, I knocked my General Organa Funko Pop down. I cursed, then said "Who gave you permission to fall?"

I grabbed a fresh cup of coffee, and dove into the next item on my agenda. "Where are you, der Bock?"

I glanced at my second computer screen, which was running the sketch our artist had created after talking to a lowlife named Cameron Grey—one of the people der Bock had conscripted to do his dirty work. Grey was just some twenty-something-year-old non-believer who had been happy to pose as Santa at Macy's and take der Bock's money to destroy kids' beliefs. Once Comet and two others had gone to confront him, the little weasel confessed everything. In no time, we knew der Bock's methods—cold hard cash for destroying someone's belief in Santa. I'd run the sketch versus my N-o-N catalog going back more than fifty years but with no results under der Bock, and too many if it could pick from any human with a ninety-five percent match or better for age and general appearance. I sighed and tweaked the parameters of my search.

There was a knock at my door. I looked up and leveled my best *I'm so over your shit* glare at…Rose, again.

"What now?" My tone was a bit more brusque than I

would've liked. But I had a sneaking suspicion I knew why she was back. "Sorry," I muttered.

"Santa is worried about you," she said. "I'm done with nice Rudolph. You need to go on vacation."

Irritated, and seeing where this was going from a mile away, I muttered, "It's not that I don't *want* to go on vacation, it's just…if I'm here then nothing…"

"You can't prevent a data breach by sheer force of will. If it were possible, you'd have achieved it years ago." She picked up a Wonder Woman action figure and turned it around in her hands.

"Hey!" I grabbed for my figure. "Give it back!"

"I was just looking at it, jeez! You are *such* a control freak sometimes." She put it down. "As I was saying, this time we have the data. All of our new non-believers are getting a package from Santa in the mail—the present they would've gotten. We'll see if it restores some belief."

"Like after the first year with the transporters versus the sleigh?" I thought back to one of my biggest triumph/failures.

She nodded. "Exactly like that. Belief bounced back when we found the kids who fell through the cracks that year. I'm hoping the same thing will happen this year. And while the elves get on that, you need to leave the Pole."

"But, Rose, I—"

Rudolph spoke, her tone serious but kind. "No, Persephone. I'm sorry to do this, but you're banned from the Pole until at least March first. I hope knowing that we booked you tickets for Boston Comic-Con—the whole con thing you like—will make you feel a little better. You can even get a hotel room instead of staying at Elf Tower because you've told me you like to do things into the late night and still get up the next morning. But for your own workaholic tendencies, we're kicking you out. And if I have to, I'll tell Liam to cut your access entirely. I understand that if you don't work, you'll die or something, but no more working *here*, and no more than two hours a day anywhere else, either. You need to store up your magic and *relax*."

I leaned back in my chair and groused, "Fine. Give me two days to finish this."

Rose raised an eyebrow at me. "Forty-eight hours. At forty-eight hours and two minutes, you need to leave or I will throw you over my shoulder and transport your antlered ass to Boston myself. Am I clear? Because you'll find 'one more thing' until the next Big Show. You need to take care of yourself. What would you say to Caity if she insisted on staying here and doing training planning and all that without a break?"

I averted my eyes and muttered "I'd tell her to leave."

"Take your own advice."

I nodded sulkily.

"Enjoy your convention," she added.

When she left, the memories flooded my brain. Memories I tried to keep in a box in the metaphorical attic because the mixture of pride and devastation was too much on a good day, much less a bad one.

I tinkered a lot as a kid, and after I saw Star Trek for the first time, I was determined to invent a transporter. I spent three years obsessively tinkering until I managed to do it on a small scale—one present from one side of the Pole to the other, on my thirteenth birthday.

My teacher brought up my project with the former Rudolph, who in turn took it to Santa. It took another three years to perfect it and increase range to the entire world. It was working so consistently by then, we used it on the night of the Big Show when I was sixteen.

I remember the excitement of that night—that my

transporter was helping Santa and the reindeer. It fizzed in my veins like champagne bubbles. I'd felt ten feet tall and invincible.

Then it all fell apart a few days later.

"We're getting letters asking us if the child writing it is on the naughty list because they didn't get a present. And belief is taking a hit, too. Sarai, the head elf on the Naughty-or-Nice team was in my office."

"Something didn't work with the transporter."

My throat had felt like someone was squeezing on it, cutting off my oxygen. This couldn't be happening. I had all those redundancies. We'd tested it worldwide using the elf towers. But it had failed. I was responsible—I had failed. I wanted to be sick.

"Mrs. Claus is leading the team to identify every child who was supposed to have gotten a present. When we find the missing kids, we'll send them a 'package' that looks like it took some abuse on the way from the post-office."

It had mostly worked. I grieved every last child who lost belief permanently because it was my fault.

Here we were again—a huge drop off in belief on my watch and because of my tech. I rubbed my temples again. Had I been too arrogant and assumed I was invincible? Phones got lost sometimes. We had been able to find or account for them all. Except one. I had assumed a phone I'd been unable to retrieve had landed in water. How had der Bock gotten his hands on it? How had he cloned it to distribute to others? I had added new tracking software and biometrics to log into a phone now. I was adding another layer of protection over the servers. But was it enough?

. . .

I retreated into my code. I worked for several more hours before I was disturbed by texts from my best friend, Wendy.

> **Big Mama: Are you coming to say goodbye or what? Or are you ghosting me?**
>
> **Zen: I'll come by soon. Just wrapping some stuff up. Rose is forcing me to leave within the next forty-eight hours.**
>
> **Big Mama: Of course you need to leave. Just promise to come back when I'm about to calve. Twins! I'm going to need your support.**
>
> **Zen: I'd never miss my honorary nieces' entrance into the world.**
>
> **Big Mama: Good. I was also texting to see if you could bring me some gingerbread. Christine is at work and I'm on stupid bedrest.**
>
> **Zen: A-ha! Your true motive appears.**
>
> **Big Mama: Dude, whatever, just bring me gingerbread.**
>
> **Zen: Did you talk to Comet like that when she was filling in for you?**
>
> **Big Mama: Of course not. She needed a kind, sweet, patient, supportive cheerleader. You've been my best friend since we were four, P. You'd**

think I was possessed by aliens if I talked to you the way I talk to her.

I smiled at my phone and promised gingerbread. I set a timer for thirty minutes, and when it went off, I dutifully went to get the baked treat. I shifted back to my true form once I shut down my laptop. The barn at Reindeer Complex had large stall/offices for all eight of Santa's reindeer. Rudolph's offices were nearby, in the same building as Santa and Mrs. Claus. They were all empty. My hooves echoed in the oppressive quiet.

Once outside, I took a deep breath of the wonderfully cold air and trotted to the bakery. I returned the bark of the little calves playing in the snow, and used my hoof to sign an autograph in the bakery. I shifted back to human to carry my bag, so when I finally got to Wendy's I could use my key.

"Wendy?"

"In the bedroom,"

No one could remember the last time a reindeer had had twins. Since human women have twins all the time without error, the doctors—elf, snowman, and reindeer—all agreed she was better off in human form until the babies were born—there was a lot of concern that she would calve too early in reindeer form.

I found Wendy surrounded by a mountain of pillows. Pillows were under her knees and behind her to raise her head. She'd have looked like a queen resting on her throne except for the frustration on her face.

"Zen! Did you bring my—"

I pulled the bag from behind my back.

"—you're the best friend a girl could hope for."

I laughed. "So what you're saying is that if I were to transport myself to France and brought you back a full case of baked goods, I could steal you away from Christine."

She snorted. "Not even for the most heavenly éclair."

"Can't blame a girl for trying," I said with a teasing wink and picked up a piece of gingerbread for myself. "So, what are we watching?"

"*Crash Landing into You*. It's a Korean soap opera."

I settled in and let her explain the plot to me. I found it soothing enough that I nodded off. When I woke up, I blinked owlishly at my friend, who had switched to reading a book.

"Morning, sunshine. That was a three-hour nap. Let me guess—you had insomnia last night."

"Every night, almost. You know that." I yawned. "But, yeah, it's been worse since the breach."

"Percy, you need to take better care of yourself."

I rolled my eyes. "So consensus seems to say."

❄

SCARLETT

I put the final touches on my friend Jeff's costume for the cosplay contest at the Boston Comic-Con. He was going to make the *best* Hawks! The wings opened to a span of eight feet, and it had taken me dozens of hours to cut, paint, and assemble the layers of "feathers." Even at my friends-and-family rate, the Hawks costume would cover any impulse buys at the upcoming

Boston Comic-Con, and the rest I could put away towards paying for San Diego Comic-Con.

Our whole friend group was going as characters from one of our favorite anime shows, *My Hero Academia*. They'd asked me to design and create all the looks and the five of us were entering the group cosplay contest. I was pinning our entry and my hopes on this. The winner of the Master level contest would get a photoshoot, and a sizeable check that would help me move to a bigger apartment where I could expand my business, once my lease was done.

I stood back and looked at my handywork hanging in a row. The three hero students' costumes for me, Grace and Felicity, hung next to Jeff's costume and wings, and Jeff's wife Carolyn's villain Dabi costume was on the other side. But it was Jeff's wings that would make it. The wings were worth every second I'd spent on them. I tried not to jinx myself, but assuming Jeff could pull off cocky, Carolyn could pull off condescending, Grace could project pure sunshine, Felicity could do what she does with microexpressions, and I could hit the right note of aggression, we had a definite shot.

I snapped a few pictures and texted them to our group chat, **BCC Approaches.**

ScarlettWitch:[picture]

ScarlettWitch: What do you think?

ScarlettWitch: The other costumes are mostly done. Felicity and Grace, lmk when you can come by for final fitting. Jeff/Carolyn you can come get your stuff anytime.

Grace: [heart-eyes emoji]

Jeff: We are not worthy. That's amazing—even better than you said.

Felicity: When are you going to give up on computers and do this full time?

ScarlettWitch: I'm happy with what I'm doing on both fronts.

Carolyn: Scarlett, they're gorgeous. Thank you!

*A*fter a few more minutes, I put my phone away with a smile. Boston Comic-Con was going to be amazing! I sat on my couch and hand sewed "pearls" onto a gown for my biggest client yet—the royal court of King Richard's Faire, the biggest Renaissance Faire in New England. The woman playing the queen had been one of my first supporters, and had recommended me for the job.

Three hours later, my body ached from sitting in one position for too long. I folded up the gown and put away the pearls, thread, pins, and needles. I stretched, and sighed with pleasure as my muscles unknotted.

I hadn't checked my mail today, preferring to stay in my apartment and my pajamas. I glanced down and decided I could go get my mail dressed this way. I yawned as I plodded down to the first level. I flipped through my mail—a request for alumni donations from MIT, a couple of credit card bills, and…ugh. My good mood was ruined. The annual Christmas card brag from my stepmother, Linda. Greeeeaaat. I can hear all about her perfect life.

Hopefully, I'd be left off the card this year—last year it had said something like *And of course we're so proud of Scarlett, who is doing well at work, but we hope she finds love.* Thanks for reducing my value to whether I've locked down a wife, Linda.

Dreading what I'd read, I poured a glass of wine. Blah blah Dad's sixth McDonald's franchise is doing well (he's underpaying his employees). Blah blah Linda's on the charity board and oh-so-important (about some endangered species she couldn't pick out of a lineup of endangered species). Allison continued to get straight A's and was a soccer star (a good kid who'd like for someone to listen when she says soccer makes her miserable).

And finally, our perpetually single Scarlett got promoted at work this year to Senior Software Engineer.

I saw red and my brain summoned up every swear word I'd ever uttered to rail against the demeaning, sexist sentence. I ground my teeth and threw the letter and the card in the trash. I'd liked it better when I thought Linda had forgotten my existence entirely and kept me out of the Christmas card loop. But no, a stamp on the back that said *I belong on the naughty list, sorry so late* reassured me that she had not forgotten me.

My mother respected my hatred for all things Christmas and didn't push me on it. However, my dad insisted I participate in all the Christmas traditions his new wife deemed necessary. Once I was eighteen, I put a stop to it. Instead, I spent Easter at their house, and thoroughly enjoyed having brunch with my little sister.

I wasn't quite sure what Linda didn't understand—it's hardly a mystery why I hate Christmas. My parents broke the news that they were getting divorced on December twenty-seventh of the year I was ten. That turned a somewhat disappointing Christmas into the death throes of my family. We hadn't even taken down the tree yet. The colorful lights were reflected in my mother's glasses as she explained that sometimes you fall out of love. Christmas was the marker I'd forever remember as the end of my family.

It was also the year I learned there was no Santa. No present. No acknowledgement. Milk and cookies and carrots exactly where I'd left them. I guess my parents were too busy lying to me about our family that they forgot about the other great lie at Christmas.

There's no such thing as Santa. Uncle Gustav's words rang in my ear.

I celebrated the worst holiday with my friends now. I'd skip all the Christmas-y stuff, but join them for dinner on Christmas Day. It started freshman year—those of us who couldn't/wouldn't go home were invited to Jeff's place for dinner. Additional members had come and gone, but our little family of five was intact and happy years after graduation.

Perpetually single Scarlett? Always the backhanded compliment with Linda. So what if I *was* perpetually single? Better than perpetually disappointed. Better to spend your time doing what you love than on the third bad date that month. Dating took way too much energy that would be better served sewing or crafting. When I closed commissions after receiving the King Richard's Faire job, I had so much costume work that there had been a six month wait list. But no, mention the promotion but stab Scarlett in the back while doing so. Typical. Not to mention…I was pretty confident I'd gone out on a disastrous date with every single bi/pan/lesbian woman in the greater Boston area, so there was no one left to date.

There's always Boston Comic-Con. Nerdy girls as far as the eye can see to lust after from a safe distance that won't get my heart trampled on.

I glanced at my calendar. Ten days left…

Pre-order the e-book HERE

For whatever reason, Kindle Direct Publishing doesn't do paperback pre-orders, sorry if that is your preferred format. But a paperback is coming.

About the Author

Delilah Night is a native Bostonian (Go Sox!) transplanted to California by way of seven years in Singapore. She grew up telling stories, including her third-grade magnum opus, The Last Unicorn (no, not *that* Last Unicorn). In high school, Delilah got very into fanfic, especially stories set in the world of Valdemar—who doesn't want their own talking horse? And in college, a former partner introduced her to erotic fanfiction—at which point Delilah put her Senior Honors Thesis aside to write some extremely dirty Star Trek: The Next Generation erotic fanfic.

In 2011, not long after the birth of her second child, Delilah wrote and had her first short story accepted for publication. Since then, she's been in a dozen anthologies from the purely fantasy—*Intrepid Horizons, Myths Monsters Mutations* to the erotic—*If Mom's Happy, Coming Together: Among the Stars.* In 2014, she traveled to Cambodia, and that trip provided the background for her first novella, *Capturing the Moment* (m/f, erotic fiction, second chances), published in 2016. In 2016, she also edited the charity anthology *Coming Together: Under the Mistletoe*, which raised money for Project Linus.

Delilah is a writer who doesn't take herself too seriously, and she hopes you'll join her as she continues down this road.

Website: www.delilahnight.com